FRESH

THE FOO

THE FOUR-PIECE

Hello, my name is Mariah Jones. I was born and raised in a small town in South Georgia called Perry, where everybody knows everybody, but sometimes the way people meet here can be very fascinating. The way I met my group of friends was one of the most enchanting encounters I've ever experienced. It was 2004, still early in the year, when I met three people that would come to be my closest friends: Deon Bradley, Shy Monroe and Rick Fuller. I met Deon first, he was a brown-skin boy with a fro and hazel eyes. My mom and his mom, Mrs. Bradley, worked together as nurses at Perry Medical Center. Deon and I went to the same school, East-wood Elementary. One afternoon my mom had to work late so Mrs. Bradley offered to pick me up and take me home with her and Deon. I stayed at the Bradley's house until my mom came to pick me up that night. During the time I spent at his house that day, Deon and I became instant friends...best friends. We played together the whole afternoon, until my mom came, and I had to leave. Every day after that I would beg to go home with Mrs. Bradley, or for Deon to come home with me, since we only stayed around the corner from each other. We spent many nights over each other's houses, and we always slept close together because Deon liked to sleep in the dark, and I was afraid of the dark.

One weekend, while Deon and I were riding our bikes to the neighborhood park, we saw a girl and a boy around our age playing basketball. Deon convinced me that we should go introduce ourselves. I wasn't open to the idea of gaining new friends because I was used to it just being the two of us, but Deon assured me that having more friends wouldn't mean that we weren't still best friends. So, we approached them, and Deon started a conversation

1

instantaneously. I didn't say much until Deon introduced us. The girl's name was Shy, but she didn't seem to have a shy bone in her body. She was a dark-skinned girl, her hair up in a curly puff who had no problem speaking her mind. The boy said his name was Richard, but he liked to be called Rick. We found out that Shy and Rick also went to Eastwood Elementary, but were in different classes. Deon joined Shy's and Rick's game of basketball while I sat on the bench and cheered from the side. The three of them played together for a while, then eventually Rick jogged over and sat beside me, and we started talking. I can't remember exactly what we talked about; but I definitely recall how I couldn't get over how light-skinned he was, his hair cornrowed to the back.

After that day in the park, the four of us spent every day after school and most weekends together. We would always hang out at either Deon's, Shy's or my house. We never went over to Rick's house because his dad was usually always at work and his mom was sick. At the time, we didn't know what she was sick from, just that it had her constantly in and out of the hospital. On the weekends, we'd ride our bikes to the fast-food joint not too far from where we all lived and buy a four-piece chicken nugget to share. It only cost a dollar, so we'd all put a quarter in for it; that somehow made sense in our seven and eight-year-old minds...we all got one nugget each. We'd buy our nuggets and bike back to the park to eat them. There was one day while we were eating our nuggets that Deon blurted out that we should call ourselves "The Four-Piece", since there were four of us and we always split a four-piece nugget. We were all in agreeance with Deon; he always had good ideas...he was a smart little fella.

A few years later, we all attended Bailey Middle School, where Rick and Shy joined the school's basketball teams, and Deon joined the band. I cheered for the city cheerleading team. Then high school came, and we all went to Memorial High School. During our freshman year is when things started to change. I convinced Shy to join the school's cheer leading team with me (she was a natural by the way), and Deon dropped band to join the football team. Rick got involved with the streets, but he never gave up basketball. Rick loved basketball, so we all knew that the streets would not get in the way of that; he had big dreams of going to the NBA.

It was during the beginning of the second semester of our freshman year that Rick's mom died of cancer. We all knew it was going to happen sooner rather than later, but everyone still took it hard. I was so afraid that the loss of his mom would push Rick into the streets more, so I decided to spend more time with him away from the four-piece to keep him focused on the right things in life. That time we spent alone really brought us closer together.

Valentine's Day of that same school year, Deon bought me the biggest stuffed teddy bear I've ever seen. I was so happy that my best friend thought of me that day. A few moments later Rick and Shy walked up. Shy was holding a gift she had received from one of her boos, and Rick came holding flowers, a box of chocolates and a black velvet jewelry box. I started to get nervous, not understanding what was about to happen. Rick gave me all the gifts, except for the jewelry box, and asked me to be his girlfriend. I dropped the teddy bear and excitedly accepted! Rick opened the jewelry box revealing a silver necklace with a green heart charm...green was his favorite color. As he went to clasp the necklace around my neck, I noticed a frown on Deon's face. I didn't understand why until I realized that I had dropped his gift to receive Rick's. I apologized to Deon many times over the next few days and he assured me that everything was all good and that he was happy that I was happy. He said he'd only frowned because he hated seeing that $50 gift sitting on the floor; he was always a jokester. After that Valentine's Day it seemed like our high school years just flew by and before I knew it we were graduating.

2015

"Deon fix your face," Mrs. Bradley said with some attitude.

The "four-piece" was posing for graduation pictures, all of us wearing our black cap and gowns and holding our red diplomas. My hair was straightened beneath my cap, my gown swallowing my petite, 5'5 form. Shy stood beside me, just a few inches taller, her long weave hanging down her back, her braces shining as she smiled. Rick stood to my other side, a tall 6'1, while Deon stood beside Shy, 5'11 with a boosie fade, his cap in his hand. I was doing a cute pose, Rick had his shades on, acting like he was shooting hoops, and Shy was making a goofy face while Deon looked at us in mock disgust.

Deon looked at us, then looked at his mom, then back at us and said, "Sorry Ma, I'm just trying to figure out why they all looking like that."

Shy punched Deon in the arm. "Shut up," she said with a laugh.

Shy's parents, along with mine and Deon's were all in attendance, grouped around the four of us while my dad set up the camera. Rick's dad was there earlier but had to leave immediately after the ceremony to get to work.

"Alright ladies and gentlemen, I think I have the camera at the perfect angle to get a group shot of us all," my dad said from where he had set the camera up on a tripod. "Now everybody say cheese," he said as he set the timer on the camera and walked over to where we all stood. We all huddled close together.

"Cheese," we all said in unison.

The camera flashed, and my dad walked over to it to check the picture. "Perfect!" he exclaimed, "I'm going to make copies of this so y'all can have it."

Our parents hugged all of us.

"I am so very proud of all four of y'all for graduating the top of your class. That is a major accomplishment!" my mom said as we all stepped out of the group hug.

The four of us thanked her in unison.

"No problem sweeties, y'all know y'all my babies," she said with a smile.

Mr. Monroe, Shy's father, placed a hand on my shoulder. "Mariah, you did a beautiful job giving your speech."

"I agree, they picked the perfect person to give the speech on behalf of the class of 2015," Mrs. Monroe added.

"Thank you so much Mr. and Mrs. Monroe," I said, hugging them both.

"Shy was looking real upset when one of the administrators came and took the beach ball she was trying to blow up," Mr. Bradley said.

Shy laughed. "I was Mr. Bradley, they always trying to shut me down for whatever reason."

"Maybe 'cause you were nominated as the class clown," Deon chimed in.

We all laughed at that.

Shy shrugged. "That could be it, I can't help it I'm a silly person."

"She gets that from her mom's side," Mr. Monroe said.

"Excuse me!" Mrs. Monroe exclaimed and pinched Mr. Monroe's arm.

"You know it's true," he said, rubbing his arm.

"Dad don't play like your side of the family got it all together, all your brothers and sisters some clowns," Shy said, making us all laugh again.

"I know y'all heard Deon sounding like me out there singing the National Anthem," Mr. Bradley said while pointing at his son.

Mrs. Bradley shook her head and rolled her eyes, "Now here you go with the foolishness." She shook her head before turning to Rick, "Richard, I am so proud of the obstacles that you overcame, it's only up from here now son."

"Thank you, Mrs. B. I appreciate that."

"Where'd your old man run off to so fast after the ceremony?" my dad asked Rick.

"Aw man Mr. J, you know how my pops is when it comes to making money...that man will work a whole 24 hours if he could," Rick responded.

My dad laughed at that.

"Yeah that is true, your dad is all about that money."

"Especially since mom passed, he's been constantly going, always trying to keep himself busy," Rick said with a sad smile on his face.

"Well I can definitely understand that," my dad said, nodding his head.

Mrs. Bradley spoke up, "Well I know if your dad could have been here he would have."

"Yes ma'am, I know, I told him that y'all would be here taking lots of pictures and stuff so he didn't feel too bad about missing the group photos. We did get to take one together before he headed out."

"Well that's good he'll have something to look back on as a memory," Mrs. Monroe said.

At that moment a guy I knew from seeing him play on the school's basketball team came running up and threw his arm around

Rick's shoulder.

"Yo Rick! Bro, I'm going to miss hooping with you man. You was something serious on that basketball court my brother."

"Appreciate that man. It was fun playing alongside you these four years."

"He was iight," Deon said sarcastically.

"Yeah, don't boost his head up anymore it's already big enough," Shy teased.

Rick laughed. "Aw man here y'all go with the hate again."

"Y'all leave my boo and his big head alone, y'all know he was the man on that court," I said, sticking up for Rick.

"Riah, I was with you until you said my head was big," Rick said looking over at me.

"It's all love baby boy, somebody gotta hate," Deon joked.

Rick nodded his head in mock understanding, "True enough, true enough."

"So Rick, I know you going off to play ball somewhere. Where you thinking about going at?" Rick's former teammate asked.

"Oh, naw bro, I'm staying here to go to Perry to hoop," Rick responded.

"Oh bet! I'm going to have to come check you out when the season starts then."

"Yeah do that. What's your next move?" Rick asked the guy.

"I'm about to go get to this money Rick. College ain't for everybody bro, so I ain't even gone waste my time going. Hell I barely made it up out of here."

"I feel that. Well whatever you do, be safe my boy," Rick said sincerely.

"That's a bet! Well I'll catch y'all later. Congratulations to all of you again," said the guy before running off.

I looked throughout our group and noticed Shy making a stank facial expression.

"Why that boy always running? Who he think he is, Forrest Gump? Anyways, I'm so glad we all decided to stay here and go to Perry University," she said, her face smoothing into a happier expression.

"That is nice that y'all decided to stay here and go to school together," Shy's mom said.

"Probably one of the best ideas I ever came up with for us," Deon said proudly.

"Boy if you don't stop with all that lying you doing," Rick responded.

"Ain't it! Always trying to take credit for something with your block head," Shy said, causing everyone to chuckle.

I stood off to the side a bit with my parent's, observing everyone. The laughter died down and my friends turned their attention to me, noticing I wasn't smiling and laughing at their banter.

Shy spoke up first, "Riah, what's wrong?"

I looked at my friends sadly before I turned to my parents.

"Mom, Dad...can we have a minute?"

"Sure sweetie." "No problem, baby." My parents responded.

My parents turned to leave, and after my friends asked their parents for some time alone, they began to leave too. Our group exchanged hugs all around before all of our parents walked off, waving goodbye as they walked to their respective cars.

My friends turned their attention back to me after their parents were gone.

"Riah, what's going on Bae?" Rick asked first.

"Yeah Riah, why you look so sad?" Deon asked next.

I couldn't help but look down at the ground, unable to meet their gazes.

"Riah, say something," Shy prompted.

I took a deep breath before lifting my head and looking at my friends.

"I have some bad news y'all."

I paused, not sure how to tell them.

"Well…?" Shy asked.

"I'm not going to college at Perry," I finally forced myself to say.

"Bih what? What do you mean you're not going to Perry?" Shy asked incredulously.

"Yeah Riah, what's going on," Deon asked.

I stood there, silently trying to figure out how to answer their questions without upsetting them.

Rick spoke before I could figure it out. Taking off his sunglasses he asked, "Bae what's up? I thought we had plans to all go to Perry?"

I sighed deeply before I spoke.

"I know we did, but I received a full ride academic scholarship to Livingston University in South Carolina. I've been going back and forth with my parents for the past two weeks over whether I should take it or not."

Their reactions were instant.

"Oh, bih turn up! Take your ass to Livingston!" Shy shouted excitedly.

Rick walked over to me and put his arm around my shoulder. "Yeah babe that's what's up fa sho!"

"I know my mama gone like that. Especially since that's where she graduated from," Shy said.

"Yeah that's cool and all, but what about the plans we had?" Deon then asked.

Shy immediately hit him in his arm, "Wow D! That was so inconsiderate of you to say."

"Yeah bro, you tripping," Rick said from beside me.

Deon raised his hands defensively.

"Calm down y'all it was a joke. Riah know that," Deon defended.

"Yeah, I know he didn't mean it like that," I said, looking at Rick and Shy.

"See," Deon rolled his eyes, "y'all all up in y'all feelings for nothing. Me and Riah good we know what to take serious and what not to take serious. I mean we did grow up together, we was a two piece before we became a four piece."

"Yeah, yeah whatever man," Rick started, "anyways, Riah don't miss the opportunity to attend the school that you been talking about going to since forever. Look man, ain't nothing going to change with us four, we all been tight since playground days and just cause you're going to be five hours away that won't get between our friendship and damn sure not gone tear up our relationship. I love you girl." Rick leaned down and kissed me on the cheek. My 5'5 self felt so short after he did that.

"Yeah Riah girl five hours ain't nothing and plus you have to come home to see your parents," Shy said.

Rick cleared his throat.

Shy looked at him then back to me. "And Rick's big head ass too."

The three of us laughed while Rick chuckled sarcastically.

"Ha ha. You so funny Shy."

"Well babe," I said looking up at my boyfriend, "your head is pretty round. I'm surprised that cap fits."

"Yeah, I bet they had to customize that bih to fit your head," Shy joked.

"Damn bro they on your ass," Deon said as he laughed along with me and Shy.

Rick shook his head at us. "They got jokes today I see. But I don't know why Riah following up Shy's ass. Let me call Mr. J to come pick her up from Memorial cause she ain't getting in my car," Rick finished with a chuckle.

I looked up at Rick, taking a small step away from him. "Dang Rick, it's like that?" I asked.

Rick pulled me back to his side, laughing. "Naw bae, you know I ain't never gonna leave you."

"Better not punk," I said, hitting Rick lightly in the side with my elbow.

"Bae," Rick paused, "I got you a graduation gift. I was going to wait until later for you to open it, but I think now is the perfect time to give it to you."

Rick unzipped his gown enough to reach into his pocket and pull out a jewelry box. He opened it to reveal a silver and green ring. It was a perfect match to the necklace he gave me back in our freshman year.

"It's a promise ring. I promise that no matter what happens, we're going to be good."

"Rick!" I exclaimed, "I love it and I love you. Thank you!"

Rick grabbed my hand and placed the ring on my ring finger. He leaned down and I met him in a kiss. I could hear Shy and Deon making gagging noises from beside us.

"Get a room freaks," Shy said loudly.

"Yeah man, don't nobody wanna see all that shit," Deon said.

We stopped kissing and both Rick and I looked at Deon and Shy before we said, "The haters! Get them off you baby," in unison. We started dusting each other's shoulders off. That got the four of us laughing.

Going to school at Livingston wasn't as bad as I thought it was going to be. I made a few new friends, but nobody compared to the four-piece. I began cheering for Livingston because I knew they had to play Perry University at least twice during the basketball season and that gave me a chance to see my man do his thing on the court. I made frequent trips home anytime that I had free time; I especially made sure to go on our anniversary and other major holidays. Sometimes the four-piece would drive to Livingston and chill with me here for a weekend. And of course, Rick made trips of his own.

Deon didn't stick with sports, he got more focused on his future career and decided to spend time job shadowing at the local Forensic Science offices as well as working with the Perry University PD. He also started dating a young lady named Jalyn. She seemed to be very sweet; we would all hangout sometimes when I would go home to Perry. Shy kept up with cheerleading like I did and joined Perry University's cheer squad. She still refused to let anyone tie her down; she had her boo's here and there. After graduation, Rick decided to cut his ties with the streets, he wanted to make basketball his main focus and he knew the streets would hold him back from fulfilling his dreams.

2017

Sophomore year of college. There's one weekend that always stuck out to me. It was Labor Day weekend and I drove back home to spend the weekend with Rick. It was a very special weekend for us, and very romantic. People would always say that we were too young to feel the way we did about each other, but that weekend changed everything, and I knew for a fact that we were meant to be. A few weeks later I got some exciting news and I couldn't wait to tell Rick. So, one Friday in November, when he was finally free from his busy basketball schedule, I was planning to tell him the news. Rick was in his dorm room with his roommates PJ, Lamar, and Jordan, who were also his basketball teammates. They were the closest members of the team from what Rick would tell me. I had a pretty good relationship with the three of them. Jordan, PJ, and Lamar were getting ready to go out, before Rick called me. They would always laugh and joke as they would tell me about the types of shenanigans, they kept going in the dorm room.

"Boy Rick get your ass up and put some muthafuckin clothes on mane and go out with us! This our first weekend off in a while and coach already gave us the go so let's go nigga," Lamar said as he walked in Rick's room wearing an all-black outfit. He was a shade or two darker than Rick and had a bald head. He stood about 5'11, the same height as Deon. Now that I think about it, he and Deon had the same husky body type as well.

Rick was sitting on his bed wearing a Perry University muscle shirt and basketball shorts and he looked over at Lamar and shook his head. "Man, I'm straight on going out tonight dawg, I'm gonna take this night off to cake on facetime with my lady. Ain't facetime her in a minute. She said she needed to tell me something important too."

"Booooy!" PJ said as he entered Rick's room, wearing blue jeans and a blue pullover sweater with brown boots. PJ was dark skinned, about 6'3, an inch or two taller than Rick and was a pretty husky built fella as well. "Do you know how soft you just sounded young blood? Man want to be on facetime with his girl all night when Club Lava bout to be full of ass and titties."

"And them big booty bitches!" Lamar exclaimed.

"Ass and titties, shake them ass and titties, ass and titties and them big booty bitches! Ayee ayeeee!" Lamar and PJ rapped together before laughing and dapping each other up.

"Oh shit! It is lady's night ain't it! What a perfect time to be off. I'm going crazy tonight y'all boys," Jordan yelled from the bathroom which was right across the hall from Rick's room.

PJ yelled back towards the closed bathroom door, "You ain't going no damn where if you don't get the fuck off the toilet ugly ass boy."

Lamar and Rick laughed hysterically at their antics.

"Boy PJ shut your ass up man, nigga can't never take a good shit without being rushed," Jordan's muffled voice responded.

"Nobody told you to overdo it tonight at the cafe and shit," PJ yelled.

"Whatever mane, I was hungry. If your fat ass wouldn't eat up all the snacks and shit a nigga wouldn't be in this predicament," Jordan said trying to plead his case.

"Yeah yeah nigga, just hurry your skinny ass up, I'm trying to get on these hoes," said PJ before he turned his attention back to Rick. "Now back to you Pretty Ricky, get your narrow ass up and put on some clothes."

Rick pointed a finger at PJ. "First of all, Big Worm, don't you ever call me Pretty Ricky again, and I already told your ass I ain't going.

I got to talk to Riah."

"Man, Rick stop being lame and fuck with your boys tonight, hell! It's lady's night, lay-deez night. These hoes gone be with the shits," Jordan yelled.

"Yeah bro," Lamar chimed in, "come on, you'll be straight with us."

"What you mean I'll be straight?" Rick asked, furrowing his brow.

"I'm just saying bro, you know niggas outside the basketball team here don't fuck with you like that," Lamar said.

"Hell yeah," PJ agreed, "and you know Avery ain't like your ass ever since you took his starting spot on the team."

"Avery was sorry as shit anyways," Jordan said, still in the bathroom.

"Like you?" Rick asked.

"Fuck you!" Jordan yelled. "You can't beat me though."

"Now Jordan," Rick began, "you know better than that. Your name shouldn't have even been Jordan, should've been something sorry like… PJ or something. I don't even know how his big ass made the team."

Rick and Lamar laughed.

"Niggas always want to talk about how big a nigga is," PJ shook his head.

"I swear y'all niggas lame man," Jordan said.

Rick chuckled. "It's all love J." Turning to look at Lamar, "But what was you saying Lamar?"

"But yeah bro, niggas be out here scheming on the low," Lamar said. "You know Perry UPD don't be patrolling like that either."

"That is true." PJ looked to Rick, "Aye Rick, what happened to that nigga D we used to room with?

Rick shrugged. "D kind of started doing his own thing like the middle of the first semester of our freshman year. Started doing work with campus PD."

"Shit man that nigga was weird as fuck anyways," PJ said, making a face.

The three of them heard Jordan laugh from the bathroom.

"That's my boy though man," Rick defended.

PJ nodded, "I feel that Rick, all I'm saying is the nigga is weird."

Lamar spoke up then. "Boy PJ shut up 'cause you look weird with all that damn blue on. Anyways Rick, you know you the man around here. I see how niggas look at you when we be walking around campus."

"They be looking at that globe on your shoulders. Big head ass boy," Jordan voiced quietly.

"Boy stop talking from the bathroom," Rick shouted, "I don't know what stinks worse your breath or your shit."

Rick, Lamar and PJ laughed loudly.

"That shit wasn't even all that funny," Jordan responded.

"Man hurry the hell up!" PJ yelled

Jordan yelled back, "Alright nigga damn!"

The three heard the toilet flush. The bathroom door opened, and Jordan walked out, wearing a white t-shirt, and blue basketball shorts. He walked over to the sinks and washed his hands before walking to his room to change his clothes. Jordan was really skinny especially compared to PJ and Lamar. He was also dark skinned and he had braces. Rick, PJ, and Jordan all had waves while Lamar had a bald head.

PJ, sounding disgusted, called out, "Damn nigga, you ain't going to take a shower and shit?"

Jordan yelled back from his room. "Shit! I ain't got time, your fat ass keep rushing me."

"You gon be like the school initials tonight in that bih," PJ said.

"The hell you talking bout?" Jordan asked.

"P-U, you stink," PJ said before he busted out laughing, Lamar and Rick cracked up too. After all their laughter died down, Jordan shouted back.

"Boooooooo!"

"Boy hurry up!" PJ yelled back.

"Yeah J let's get it," Lamar yelled towards Jordan's room. He turned back to Rick. "So, what's up Rick, you sliding with us or...?"

"Naw bro," Rick shook his head, "I'm good on it, it's already past 12 anyways so that mean we wouldn't even get to Lava till about 12:30."

"Nigga," PJ interjected, "shit don't get popping till 12:30 at Lava anyways and you should know that since you from here."

"Don't matter bro," Rick responded, "I ain't going! Now don't ask me no more. I got some work to catch up on anyways, Dr. Reynolds been cutting me some slack with this schoolwork."

"Alright, alright I ain't gone ask you no more little Richie Rich," PJ said while pinching Rick's cheek and laughed.

Rick smacked PJ's hand off his cheek and said, "You got jokes tonight huh fat boy."

PJ laughed and said, "You know how I do," he stopped laughing then looked at his phone and said with aggravation in his voice, "Damn man!".

Lamar and Rick both looked at PJ staring at his phone then Rick asked, "What happened P?"

PJ looked up from his phone shaking his head and said, "Lacy's ass just text me."

Lamar asked, with disgust in his voice, "You still messing with that crazy chick?"

"Yeah man, that crazy shit do something to me," PJ said with a big grin on his face.

"Shawty look like a killer wearing black all the time," Lamar responded.

"Shit I don't give a damn what color she be wearing to be honest, she don't be in them clothes for long anyways," PJ explained.

Rick laughed at his two roommates' comments then looked at PJ and asked, "Well what did she say P?"

"Say she wants to come through tonight, I told her I'm going to Lava with y'all. Bih said she'll wait on me to get back," PJ said.

"You a wild man P," Rick responded.

"Get it how you live my boy, Lacy got that splash," PJ said.

"Yeah she do," Lamar chimed in.

"Might as well go'on move her ass too Rick, shit. You know she love her some basketball meat," PJ said to Rick.

"Boy hell naw. I am definitely straight on that shit," Rick responded. That's what he better had said if he knew what was good for him.

PJ laughed at Rick's response then noticed the outfit that Lamar was wearing and said, "You talking about Lacy wearing all black and your ass standing there looking like 11:59 PM."

Lamar laughed then said, "Boy shut your ass up over there looking like…"

Before Lamar could finish his statement, Jordan walked into the room wearing a black pull over sweater, gray joggers and black tennis shoes. He stood in Rick's doorway with a bottle of alcohol in his hand.

"Alright niggas I'm ready to slide up out of here, but before we go you already know what time it is." Jordan tapped the bottle of alcohol and smiled big, showing his braces.

PJ looked Jordan up and down in disgust then shook his head. "Fuck that Lamar, look at this nigga here. Close your mouth before you blind somebody, shiny mouth boy." Everybody, except Jordan, laughed at PJ's comment.

"Nigga shut y'all asses up and check y'all watches," said Jordan. Rick, PJ, and Lamar stopped laughing and each looked at their wrists then all four in unison shouted, "Shot thirty!"

Rick got up from his bed and walked to his desk. He pulled four shot glasses from the drawer and gave each of his roommates one. Jordan poured alcohol in each of their glasses and they each took their shots. They poured up 3 more rounds after that. After they all took their last shot Jordan went to go put the bottle of alcohol back in his room then came back to Rick's room to dap him up. PJ dapped Rick up too before he and Jordan made their way out the door to head out to Lava. Lamar stayed behind to talk to Rick some more.

"Rick man be safe tonight, you know we move together, and I don't want to leave you here by yourself," Lamar said.

"I'm going to be good mane, I told you I gave up that street lifestyle way before I came to Perry so any beef shit I had with anybody should be dead by now you feel me," Rick responded.

Lamar nodded in agreement to Rick's statement and said, "I feel you bro, but you know some niggas can't let shit go. Just be careful tonight my boy and keep the door locked."

"I will fa sho bro," Rick responded.

Rick and Lamar dapped each other up and Rick walked Lamar to the front door and locked it behind him. Just as Rick made his way back to his room there was a bang on the door. He opened the door and it was Lamar. Lamar told Rick that he didn't have his key and he left his black skully in his room. Lamar walked back to his room to get the things that he left and Rick made his way back to his room to call me. Lamar grabbed his things then made his way back out the front door, telling Rick bye again as he passed his room.

I was in my dorm room at Livingston, in the process of folding some laundry on my bed, when my MacBook started ringing. I looked over and noticed that it was Rick calling so I stopped folding clothes and made my way to the desk where my laptop was and answered the call. When I answered I saw my handsome boyfriend sitting at his desk putting his headphones in his computer then putting the ear buds in his ears. There was a folder sitting in front of him like he was about to do some work or something. I smiled at him and said, "Hey Bae."

"Sup baby girl, what you up to?" he responded.

"Nothing much, folding these clothes I shoulda been folded last week," I said.

"Girl you need to do better," Rick said shaking his head.

I sucked my teeth then said, "Boy hush cause I know that laundry basket of yours running over."

"Damn you right," he said as he looked over at his laundry basket in a corner of his room and noticed that it was full of dirty clothes.

"Same Ole Rick," I said laughing and shaking my head. I stopped laughing then just stared at him before I said, "Boy look at you over there looking how you looking. You look good."

"Oh, you like what you see?" he asked.

"Yes! You is fine boy," I said laughing a little.

"Ain't no boy over here girl, this all man," he said flexing his muscles in the camera.

I laughed more at that. "Boy please. Can't never give light skin niggas complements without it going to their head. And you know you don't need any more complements 'cause that thing on your shoulders is huge."

"You don't say nothing about my head being huge when it be between your legs," he said while flicking his tongue at me.

I put my hand over my mouth and laughed. "Boy hush. Don't be saying that all loud like that while your roommates there."

He laughed and said, "Hush girl, all them boys went to Lava tonight."

"All of them went?" I asked.

"Yup," he answered.

"Oh ok. Why didn't you go out with them? Y'all ain't got a game or practice this weekend," I asked.

"I told them boys I wanted to stay in tonight and cake up on facetime with you."

"Awwww Rick you're so sweet," I smiled.

He looked at me and winked, "Yeah Bae, we rarely get to facetime like that anymore with me having late practices and you having to get up early for your job and shit. I miss your beautiful face."

"I miss you too Bae. Thanksgiving is two weeks away and I have a whole week off so we are definitely spending that weekend before and that week together," I said.

"That's a bet, I think we got a game that Tuesday then we got the rest of the week off," he said.

"Cool, well I will definitely be at the game Tuesday screaming my lungs out like I was two weekends ago when y'all played that school down the road from me. What's the name of that school again?" I asked.

"You talking about Braxton State," he answered.

"Yeah that's it. They were a pretty good team," I said.

"Yeah they was, but not good enough cause we still beat they ass," Rick said proudly.

I sucked my teeth. "Y'all only won because I was there."

Rick sat back in his desk chair. "Is that right?" he asked.

I laughed, "Hell yeah."

Rick started laughing too. "I hear you. You should have brought your ass to the game we lost against Morrison, then we could have still been undefeated."

I shrugged my shoulders. "Whelp babe you can't win them all."

"True enough," he said in agreement.

Rick eventually pulled out a book and sat it on his desk then started flipping through the pages. He stopped on the page he was looking for, pulled some paper out of the folder and started writing.

"What kind of work are you about to start working on?" I asked.

"This damn Biology work I was supposed to been do."

"Why you ain't been done it Rick?" I asked with a stern voice.

"I ain't really have time Riah. Thankfully Mrs. Reynolds's son is on the team, so she already knows what the fuck going on."

"Well that's good I guess. Turn it in on time from now on or I'm going to knock that boulder off your shoulders," I said.

He looked up from his book at me, laughed and said, "Riah, one thing I ain't worried about is you doing that."

I made a fist with my hand then held it to the camera. "You better be!"

Rick laughed a little and raised one eyebrow. "Why is that?"

"Baby, 'cause I'm a thug!" I rapped back to him.

He leaned back in his chair, laughing, "Girl you far from a thug."

I sucked my teeth, laughed and said, "You a hater man."

"Whatever you want to call it Bae." We both laughed together before Rick went back to looking through his textbook.

I started fiddling with things on my desk. "Hey!" I exclaimed.

Rick looked up from his book. "What's up?"

"When the last time you heard from D?" Rick looked up, then started scratching the side of his face. "Shit I hit D up like Wednesday or Thursday of last week."

"Sheesh why has it been so long? Y'all used to talk every day."

"I know Bae, but D be doing his own thing. That internship he doing with the Perry campus Police Department takes up most of his time. Boy gonna be out here solving mysteries after a while."

I chuckled. "Yeah true. Shy told me she sees him every day, riding around with campus police. You know, ever since we were little, he used to call himself Deon Holmes."

"That's what I'm saying. I mean, ain't no issue between me and D, but I can tell that things have changed between us, especially since we couldn't be roommates this year. It seems like we also started losing touch a little more after he and Jalyn broke up. With my hectic basketball schedule, I couldn't really be there for him as much during that time. It's like he started honing in on work a little more."

"Yeah, that makes sense. Well I mean, he still acts the same towards me and Shy. He hits both of us up every day. And I know he and Jalyn were rocking pretty hard for a while, so even though he plays hard when we try to talk to him about it, I am sure it's a little rough," I said.

"I don't know what his problem is or whatever. I wish the best for bro 'cause he got me out of plenty jams when I was in them streets," Rick responded.

"I don't think it is a problem, I think he just wants you to focus because he knows how much basketball means to you. When I last talked to him he said that he was going to plan a trip with just the four-piece as soon as the basketball season was over."

"That's real, a trip with the crew would be nice man. Me and Shy ate lunch together this past Wednesday at the spot," Rick told me.

"Yeah, she told me, did y'all get the usual?" I asked.

"Did."

"I'm definitely going there when I come down for Thanksgiving," I said.

"True. I'm gone hit D up tomorrow and see if he wants to grab drinks or something tomorrow night," Rick said.

"Might as well tell Shy's crazy ass to tag along too," I said with a smirk.

"Yeah Ima hit that goofball up too. Every time I see her she always yells out 'Richie Rich!' I just put my head down and keep walking. I be seeing her with some big girl now." Rick said, laughing and shaking his head.

"Rick!" I exclaimed.

"What Bae? She is a little on the big side," Rick said while holding in a laugh.

It took everything not for me to laugh at that fool. I gathered myself before responding, "So? Rick, that's still not nice to say."

Rick laughed even more, "Look at you, trying not to laugh. It's not like I call the girl big to her face or nothing."

"I hear you Mr. Fuller," I said, rolling my eyes at him.

"Good to know Mrs. Fuller," he responded.

"Mrs. Fuller huh?" I asked, raising an eyebrow.

"Yup, act like you know."

"I mean, I don't know since my hands are kind of bare," I said holding both of my hands up in the camera for him to see.

He examined both of my hands, "Where the promise ring I got you at?"

I picked the ring up from next to my laptop and showed Rick.

"Right here. I took it off when I washed my hair earlier and didn't put it back on because I started washing dishes," I explained.

"Oh, I was about to say. But yeah, it's about time to replace that ring with a better one," Rick said, smiling at me.

I stared back at him. "Is that right?"

He stared back at me with those brown eyes, just smiling, "Yup, that's right."

I couldn't do anything but smile back at him. "I like the sound of that."

"I knew that you would," Rick responded.

"I love you, big head."

"Dang so you got the right to talk about people, but I don't? Pure blasphemy," he said.

I laughed, "You can't do what I do boy."

"Here you go with that boy mess again," Rick said, shaking his head.

"My bad, 'man'."

"That's more like it," he laughed, "I love you too."

"Whatever Richard Fuller," I responded sarcastically then laughed. I started playing with the necklace Rick got me for Valentine's Day back in our freshman year of high school. I found myself admiring how beautiful it was and it brought back many of our past memories.

"I see you still rocking that necklace I got you when I asked you to be my girlfriend," Rick said as he watched me play with the charm.

I looked into his eyes and smiled, "Of course, only time I take it off is when I shower. I barely want to take it off then but I don't want to mess it up."

"Yeah, don't let it rust from the shower. Green, brown and silver won't look good together," he responded.

"You right about that," I said. I then looked at the time in the bottom corner of my computer. "Hey babe hold on real quick, I have to go grab my clothes out of the dryer. They should be done by now."

"What time did you put them in there?" he asked.

"Like 12 on the dot."

"Oh yeah they should be good and done by now. It's like 1:07," Rick said.

"Right, so let me go grab them and I'll be right back," I said.

"Don't be having me waiting long," he said looking at me.

I squinted my eyes at him… "Or what?"

"Try me and see."

"Blah blah." I stuck my tongue out at him as I got up out of my desk chair. I started walking really slow towards the door before Rick told me to put a pep in my step. I laughed and sped up and walked out of my dorm. I made my way down the hall to the laundry room, which wasn't too far from my dorm, to grab my clothes. Thankfully they were done, those dryers never seemed to be working. I grabbed all of my clothes out the dryer, put them in my basket and made my way back to my room. When I got back I called out to let Rick know I was back in the room then I put my basket of clothes on the floor and started to fold the clothes on my bed.

"Been eating good haven't you girl?" Rick asked. I looked in the direction of my laptop on my desk. I could see Rick watching me through the screen. "What you mean?"

"Looking a little thick over there," he said.

"Oh yeah…" I said as I stopped folding my clothes and made my way over to the desk. I sat down in the chair and said, "I been wanting to tell you since last week, but you been so busy. But since you was off this weekend I figured this would be the perfect time to tell you."

Rick put down his pencil and looked me in my eyes, "Tell me what Riah?"

I sighed. "Well Rick..." While I was getting ready to finish my statement I noticed somebody walk past Rick's open door. "Rick?" I said in a slightly scared voice.

"What's up?"

"I thought you said your roommates were out."

Rick raised an eyebrow at me. "They are, why you say that?"

"Because I just saw somebody wearing all black walk past your room," I replied.

Rick turned around in his chair and yelled out "Yo!" in the direction of the hallway. There was no response. Rick turned back around to face his desk and shrugged his shoulders, "It was probably this girl name Lacy, she's one of PJ's freaks. He did say that she would be coming by to wait on him to get back from Lava. She tends to come by and wait on him a lot when he's not here."

"It just kind of caught me by surprise that's all," I said with relief.

"No worries baby girl, ain't nobody going to fuck with big Rick! 'Cause I'm the man round here!" Rick yelled out.

"Here you go," I laughed and shook my head. I stood up from my chair and walked backed over to my bed to finish folding clothes. As I was walking back to my bed Rick shouted out, "Damn Riah!" I turned around to look at the laptop. "What?"

"That ass fat girl," he responded with a laugh.

I laughed a little, bent over then said, "Oh is it?" I could see Rick staring hard at me through the screen while I bent over.

"Hell yeah," he said. I stood up and laughed as I made my way back to the computer

"Man, Rick you got me off track from telling you the good news," I sat down in the chair.

Rick laughed. "What's the exciting news Bae?"

"Well Rick-" I was cut off by what sounded like pots and pans hitting the floor on Rick's end. Rick took one of his ear buds out of his ear and turned around in his chair to face the doorway. I stared at Rick, starting to feel a little scared. "Rick, what the hell was that noise?"

"I don't know what that could have been," Rick said in a very soft voice. The noise happened again while we were both still looking at the door.

"There it is again! Rick what is that?" I asked in a more scared voice.

"I don't know, but I'm gone go check it out."

"Be careful," I replied with concern.

"I got you," he said as he took his headphones completely off and placed them on his desk. Rick got up from his chair and walked out of his room toward the direction of where the noise came from. It was quiet for a few seconds before I heard muffled noises through Rick's headphones, as they were barely picking up the sounds. I called out for Rick, but he couldn't hear me because his headphones were still plugged in. It felt like a million thoughts began running through my head a mile per minute. The feeling of terror began kicking in, and I felt stifled by my fears as I thought about what could possibly be going on. My anxiety is soaring through the roof, and my heart is pounding; I can literally feel every ounce of blood rushing from my head to my toes. Questions going through my head…

Where is he?

Why isn't he coming back to the room?

WHAT is going on?

The muffled sounds suddenly stopped, and it became quiet. The silence is killing me! I grew more worried and concerned the longer I stared at the door through the computer screen. Then I saw Rick slowly make his way back to the room. He was leaning against the doorframe, holding his lower stomach and neck. I could tell that he was clearly hurt. I heard him say something, but I couldn't make it out. I frantically called his name over and over, banging my desk, begging him to unplug the headphones so I could hear him better. He seemed to gather his strength as he pushed off the doorframe and tried to walk over to his desk. He walked slowly and stumbled with every step he took. As he got closer I realized his hands were covered in blood.

"Rick! What happened?" I screamed out. He still couldn't hear me.

"Call the police. Riah, I love you …" I faintly heard Rick say before he fell to the ground. He didn't get back up. The tears came suddenly, and I laid my head down on my desk. I couldn't get them to stop, no matter how much I tried to convince myself that Rick was alright. When I lifted my head, I looked back at the computer screen and saw the person dressed in all black walking toward the computer. They were wearing a black ski mask. They closed Rick's laptop and my screen went black, the video call ending.

I sat there in disbelief, staring at the home screen of my computer; it felt like everything was moving in slow-motion. I frantically grabbed my phone to call the police, Rick's dad, Shy, and Deon, in that order, to tell them what just happened.

My thoughts were all over the place.

I can't believe I had just watched the love of my life die right in front of my eyes. This has to be a dream, this can't be the way we end…the way he ends! Rick still has his whole life ahead of him; he still has to graduate from college and go to the NBA. Rick doesn't want to let his dad down or disappoint his mom; she's the reason behind him working so hard. How is Mr. Fuller going to take the news? First his wife and now

Anthony Taylor

his only child?

The police better find that bitch who did this to Rick. Rick may have had a dangerous past, but that was years ago, so why would anyone want to hurt him? I didn't even get to tell him the news. Who would've ever thought that being long distance lovers would come to mean Rick loving me from heaven? My heart is in pieces. I think I'm on the verge of a panic attack, but I have to stay strong and I have to stay calm, for the baby's sake. I can't let anything happen to our baby, so that I will always have a piece of Rick with me. I want to head to Perry tonight, but I know I'm not mentally stable enough to make that five-hour drive. I'll leave first thing in the morning.

THE AFTERMATH

Rick's death didn't take long to make the local news stations and even some of the surrounding counties' news stations. It was about one o'clock, a chilly afternoon of the next day, when I arrived at Perry University. I was supposed to be meeting Shy by Rick's housing building where I could hopefully find someone who could tell me what happened. I parked my 2010 Honda Accord in the parking lot outside of the building, got out and made my way in the direction of his dorm. I saw Shy standing with PJ, Jordan, and Lamar outside of Rick's building wearing a pink, black and white jogging suit. They were all wearing their clothes from the night before because they weren't allowed to enter the room until officials had finished investigating the crime scene.

I started to walk faster and when Shy saw me walking up she came to meet me the rest of the way and pulled me into a tight hug. And soon as we had our arms around each other we both began to cry in disbelief over the event of last night. Through my tears I saw PJ walking up to me and Shy. I let her go and met him for a hug. I planted my face in his chest while he rubbed my back.

"Mariah, I'm so sorry about what happened to Rick last night. You know if I could've, I would have stopped that shit from happening." PJ said in a comforting voice. I couldn't even say anything because I was crying so hard on his chest.

Jordan made his way over to us and started rubbing my back too. "Mariah, you know we got you. Rick was like our brother, so whatever you need we got you. We gone get through this together sis."

PJ and I stop hugging and my tears finally slowed down enough for me to speak.

"I really appreciate y'all, I just can't believe somebody would do this to Rick," I said, still sniffling a little.

"Me neither man, shit is crazy," Jordan said, shaking his head and wiping his hand down his face.

PJ ran his hand over his head. "Hell yeah it is. Didn't know last night would be the last time we would see Rick."

"Yeah man shit mind boggling. Have y'all seen D yet?" Jordan asked me and Shy.

I shook my head, "I texted him when I got here, he said that he had to check in at the station and wanted to see if he could get some inside intel on the case."

"Okay cool." Jordan responded.

"Lamar, what's good?" Shy said to Lamar who was still standing near the building, looking at the ground. We all turned our attention to him and saw how puffy his eyes were and the hurt look on his face once he lifted his head. He stared at us for a minute, then snapped, "Fuck man! It's my fault man, it's my fault!" he yelled, punching the bulletin board next to him. We all stood there looking at him in confusion.

"What do you mean it's your fault?" I asked him.

"Yeah bro, what you mean it's your fault?" PJ chimed in. Me, PJ, Shy and Jordan slowly made our way over to Lamar. His eyes were full of tears.

"I forgot to tell Rick to lock the door behind me after I went back in the room to get my hat," Lamar said, sniffling and pointing at the hat on his head. "If the door was locked then nobody would've been able to come in. It's all my fault" he paused, "all my fucking fault man." We finally made it to where he was standing and I walked up to him to hug him while PJ, Jordan, and Shy stood back.

"It's not your fault Lamar, any other time y'all leave the door unlocked. How could you have known this time would have resulted in something like this," I tried to comfort him.

"Yeah bruh, relax, don't beat yourself up for what somebody else did." PJ chimed in. Just as PJ was finishing his statement, Officer Anderson and Forensics Specialist, Agent Philips walked over from the direction of the boys' dorm, both dressed in tan trench coats and black pants. Officer Anderson was a 5'9, chubby white guy with a beard and bald head who worked for the Perry University Police Department and Agent Philips was a 5'8, skinny brown-skinned guy. They both waved at us before Officer Anderson asked the boys, "Gentlemen, did you get the rest of your belongings out of the room?"

"No sir, we were waiting on you two to come so we could get more information on what really happened," Jordan answered.

"The only information that we can provide you is what was said on the news, everything else is confidential," said Agent Philips, walking in closer to us.

"So y'all can't even tell his girlfriend, Mariah?" PJ replied in a stern voice.

"It's confidential, Perceval," Officer Anderson responded back to PJ in a stern voice.

"Aye man you don't know me like that to be calling me by my government name. We just trying to find out what happened to my dawg," PJ said offensively.

"We understand, but like we stated it is confidential information," Agent Philips said.

"Confidential my ass! His fucking girlfriend is right here, she got the right to know something," PJ said, pointing at me while still facing Officer Anderson and Agent Philips.

I placed my hand on PJ's shoulder, trying to soothe him, "Calm down PJ, I saw a little bit of what happened. I know what's up."

"Mariah!" Shy said sternly as she stepped closer to me. I looked at her and I realized that I might have said something that the officers didn't know.

"Excuse me ma'am, did you just say that you witnessed the events of last night?" Officer Anderson asked.

I turned to look at him and nervously said, "Yes sir, I was five hours away in my dorm room at Livingston University. We were using Facetime on our laptops, and I witnessed part of his death." Agent Philips pulled out a pen and note pad and started taking notes.

Officer Anderson looked at me with a confused look on his face, "Laptop? There was no laptop on the scene, only a cellphone."

"Huh? What you mean? There has to be a laptop in there because that's what we were talking on," I replied, trying not to get mad.

"This some straight bullshit! So y'all mean to tell me y'all don't even have all y'alls evidence together?" Lamar said angrily. All hell broke loose then, we all started shouting different things at the officers.

Our shouts of anger went on for a while until Officer Anderson tried defusing the situation. "Calm down everyone! We will get to the bottom of this." We all lowered our voices to listen to what he had to say, "In the meantime, let's let you boys get your belongings. And to the young lady..." Anderson said while snapping his fingers.

"Mariah!" PJ said in a frustrated voice.

"Yes, to Ms. Mariah and you three young men, we will need to have further discussions with you all down at the station," Officer Anderson said while reaching into his trench coat pocket to pull out his card, "no later than tomorrow afternoon please," he held out a card for each of us to take.

"Okay," I said as I hesitantly to a card.

Agent Philips and Officer Anderson led the way back to the boys' dorm while we all followed. I pulled Officer Anderson to the side before he made his way into the room while everyone else walked in behind Agent Philips.

"Yes?" Officer Anderson looked at me and asked.

"Is it possible that I can get Rick's phone out of his room?" I asked with a sad expression on my face. He saw the expression on my face then looked inside the room to make sure Agent Philips wasn't paying attention to us.

He turned back to face me, bent over and whispered, "I'm not supposed to let you in that room, but be quick."

I mouthed a thank you to him as we made our way inside the dorm. He stood outside of Rick's doorway while I went under the caution tape barring the doorway. When I got inside of the room I stood there in shock taking in the sight of the blood stains on the floor.

"Wow Rick, this really happened," I said softly to myself, covering my mouth with my hand. Officer Anderson saw me just standing there and cleared his throat snapping me out of it and reminding me that I didn't have much time. I started to look for the phone, stepping over blood so I wouldn't get any on my shoes. I saw the phone laying on the desk, where Rick's laptop should have been, amidst the rest of some of his belongings. I grabbed it, put it in my hoodie pocket and made my way back out of the room, telling Officer Anderson thank you again as I passed by him.

Shy and I lent a helping hand to PJ, Jordan and Lamar in packing the stuff up from their rooms and loading it into their cars. It didn't take us long at all, they didn't really have that much to pack up. Once we got the last bit of their things loaded, Shy and I said our goodbyes to the boys and they left to move into their new room. We decided to head to our favorite lunch spot to grab something to eat. I texted Deon when we got in my car telling him to meet us there whenever he got done with his errands.

It didn't take long to get to the restaurant and we were seated in a booth near from the front door. Our waitress walked over to our table, wearing her all black outfit, not even two minutes after we sat down asking if we were ready to order. She was a 5'6 brown-skinned, curvaceous young lady that had long curly hair.

"How y'all ladies doing today?" she said with a pen and pad in her hands. Shy and I both answered "fine," in unison.

"Good, well my name is Lacy and I will be taking care of you all today. What can I start y'all off with to drink?"

"I'll take a water," Shy answered.

"I'll take a water as well," I said.

"Okay and are y'all ready to order now or do you need a few minutes?" Lacy asked.

"Well we are expecting one more person so we'll wait until he gets here," Shy answered.

"Okay no problem. I'll grab those waters for y'all now and be right back." Lacy said. Shy and I both thanked her and Lacy walked off to go grab the drinks.

"She is so pretty," Shy said as she watched Lacy walk off.

"Yeah she is."

"I hate the fact that she is making a name for herself though," Shy said, looking back at me and shaking her head.

"Making a name for herself how?"

"Baby just lost her virginity back in August and now it's damn November and she done slept with everybody on the basketball team."

"Damn everybody?" I asked with concern in my voice.

"Everybody except for Rick, I shut that shit down before it got started," she laughed. "She hooked on PJ big ass for whatever reason."

I laughed a little, "That must be the girl Rick was telling me about."

"What he said girl?"

"Last night, he was just like…it's this girl that PJ messes with on a regular that pops up at their room and just waits on him."

"Child I'm sure that's who he was talking about," Shy shook her head. "PJ probably be squishing the poor girl."

"Shy, PJ is not all that big."

"Girl yes he is, coach needs to put him in the game more and maybe he'll slim up."

"Stop," I said laughing.

"Girl for real," Shy said as her laugh combined with mine. Our laughter died down.

"But aye?" Shy asked.

"What's up?"

Shy looked around the restaurant then leaned over the table and whispered, "Do you think Lamar killed Rick?"

I looked at her with a perplexed look on my face, "No, why would you think that? Rick and Lamar were the closest on the team, on and off the court."

"Well I'm just saying, shit seems a little fishy," Shy said as she leaned back in her seat.

"Where are you getting this assumption from Shy?"

"Girl didn't you say you saw Rick's killer with a black skully over their face?"

"Yeah, but it was more like a ski mask," I replied, confused.

"Girl same shit, but didn't Lamar say that he went back to the room specifically for his black skully?"

"But…" I stopped, thinking to myself before speaking again, "It can't be Lamar, the way he was crying outside the building seemed so genuine."

"Girl that was probably just an act to cover his ass."

"Mmm, I don't know Shy."

"Well girl it's just something to think about."

The door to the restaurant opened right after Shy finished her statement and we both looked in the direction of the door and saw Deon walking in. He was standing there in a nice collared shirt on with khakis, scanning the restaurant for us. It was so good to finally see my friend, he looked good as he walked in looking so professional. Shy threw her hand up in the air and called his name. He turned to look at us and walked over to our table. When he got to the booth he leaned over and gave Shy a hug before sitting down beside me and giving me a hug.

"What's up y'all? Sorry I couldn't make it to Rick's room earlier I had to handle some things at the station. Please forgive me," he said.

"No problem, I'm glad you're here now though," I said, smiling at him. "Were you able to find out anything at the station?" I asked.

"Unfortunately, they are still working on gathering all of the evidence, and there wasn't much in Rick's file," Deon said. He looked down at the ground before taking a deep sigh, "This entire ordeal is so unbelievable...I am so crushed." He grabbed my hand as a means of comfort, and said, "We'll get through this though."

Lacy walked back to our booth with two waters in her hand. She placed a water in front of me then placed one in front of Shy.

"What's up Lacy?" Deon said with a smile.

"Hey Deon, how are you? Sorry to hear about Rick. PJ texted me and told me what happened before I saw it on the news. That's sad man," Lacy replied. Shy and I looked at each other with crazy expressions on our faces when she said Rick's name.

"I'm good man and I appreciate that. This is Rick's girlfriend Mariah," Deon said, putting his hand on my shoulder.

"Oh hey, sorry for your loss," Lacy said, smiling at me.

"Thank you," I replied.

"No problem," she turned her attention back to Deon, "What can I get you to drink Deon?"

Deon looked at Shy and I, "Bruh, why didn't y'all get me anything to drink?"

"Because D, you always switching up every time we come here," Shy answered.

"Whatever man," he sucked his teeth and looked at Lacy, "let me get a Sprite."

"Okay I'll be right back with that." Lacy turned to head towards the kitchen.

"Hold on Lacy," Deon called out. He looked at me and Shy, "I know what y'all want, we eat the same thing every time we come here."

"You right," I said looking at Deon. I looked at Lacy, "We are all going to have the 10-piece hot wing combo with lemon pepper sprinkles on the wings and fries, and a large order of mozzarella sticks."

"And don't forget the ranch. When me and Rick came here Wednesday our waiter forgot to bring us some," Shy added.

"Them cheese sticks be real good," Deon said.

Lacy wrote our order down. "Alright y'all, I will be back with all of that soon. Shouldn't take too long." She walked off towards the kitchen.

"Soooo, how do you know Lacy?" Shy asked Deon, squinting at him suspiciously. I looked at him waiting for him to answer Shy's question.

"Who don't know Lacy hot ass," he said laughing.

Shy started laughing with him, "You right."

"Dang baby girl really out there like that?" I asked.

"Yeah man it's crazy, and to be real, it ain't even all that good, I only had it once and I was straight on her after that," Deon said shaking his head.

"Deon! You too?" Shy asked as she laughed and slapped the table.

"Yeah it ain't that serious, I just wanted to see what all the hype was about," he answered in a cunning voice.

I shook my head, "Deon I'm disappointed, never thought you would be the one to have everyone's sloppy seconds."

"Damn Mariah you sounding like me with the comebacks," Shy chuckled.

"Riah really?" Deon said, a disgusted look on his face.

"I'm just saying," I replied, shrugging my shoulders.

"Damn Mariah, that kind of hurt my feelings," he said, leaning away from me.

"Come on, Deon don't be like that," I said as I leaned over to him to hug his neck, "you know I was just playing."

Shy looked at us like we were crazy, "Really Riah, you always sucking up to Deon block head ass." I playfully rolled my eyes at Shy then went back to my side of the booth.

"Shy you just hating cause Riah closer to me than you," Deon said, sticking his tongue out at her. Shy stuck her fingers in her water then flicked some at Deon, "Shut up D, ain't nobody jealous."

"Y'all stop, you know I love both of y'all equally," I said, laughing a little. We all laughed together. Our laughter slowly died down and there was a brief silence at the table.

My cellphone vibrated in my pocket with a text notification, I pulled it out and saw it was from Rick's dad.

"Mr. Fuller just texted me, he wants us all to stop by when we leave here."

Deon and Shy both nodded and said okay.

"Damn it's weird us all being here without our boy Rick," Deon said.

"Yeah man for real," Shy added. There was an awkward silence. I looked down, looking at the picture of me and Rick on the wallpaper on my phone.

"Mariah you can crash with me tonight if you want. You know I don't have any roommates," Deon said.

I lifted my head and looked at him, "Okay, I'll do that. Let me text my parents and let them know I'll see them tomorrow." I looked back down at my phone to text my parents.

"Damn, Riah get an invite and I don't?" Shy said playfully. Deon was about to answer back but Lacy was walked up with his drink.

"Here's your drink, y'alls food will be out shortly," she said after placing Deon's drink on the table in front of him.

"Thanks," he said.

"No problem," she said, and she walked back to the kitchen. Deon grabbed his straw, put it in his drink, took a sip then said, "It don't matter Shy."

"It don't matter? It's a yes or no question nigga." Shy replied.

"Yes, Shy, you can crash at my spot too," Deon said as he huffed out a breath.

"Now was that so hard?" she asked with a big smile on her face, showing her pink braces.

I laughed at my friends and their silliness. I noticed Lacy walking over to us with our food in her hands. She placed all of our food down in front of us. We ate and chatted, enjoying each other's company. When we all finished eating our food Lacy brought out the checks and Deon paid for everyone's meal. We left the restaurant and the three of us made our way to Mr. Fuller's house. Shy and I rode in my car, and Deon tailed us in his.

About thirty minutes later we arrived. We parked the cars then walked to front door together, and Deon rang the doorbell. Mr. Fuller opened the door shortly after, wearing his work clothes and house shoes. His eyes were glossy and swollen from crying, but he still managed to put on a smile for us. It was kind of hard for me to look at him at first; Rick favored him so much, from head to toe.

"Hey Kids, come on in," he said as he motioned for us to come in. He hugged each of us as we walked inside. He closed the door behind us.

"Pops, how have you been holding up?" I asked.

He took a deep breath. "The best I can baby girl, what about you?"

I shook my head. "Not good at all honestly, but I'm forcing myself to hold it together."

"Yeah, I completely understand," he turned to Shy and Deon, "What about y'all?"

They both nodded at him and said that they were okay.

"That's good," he said then cleared his throat, "the reason I wanted y'all to come over today is to help me with the funeral arrangements."

"So soon?" Shy asked.

"I just wanted to go ahead and get it handled. The thought of planning my boy's funeral is a lot to deal with and I don't want to drag it out any longer than I have to."

"I understand," Shy said.

"Well, y'all follow me to the dining room and let's get started," Mr. Fuller said as he started making his way to the kitchen. We followed him to the dining room, sat at the table and he continued, "I have gotten in contact with the funeral home down the road; that's where Rick is now, they will be the ones we will be dealing with."

"I think Rick should be dressed in a white tux with a green handkerchief and everyone in attendance should wear either green or white," I said. I paused, thinking about Rick while holding the necklace he bought me in my hand. I smiled, "Green was his favorite color, he would want it that way." Everyone nodded and agreed. Mr. Fuller started writing things down in the note pad that laid on the table in front of him.

"Sounds good, Deon do you think you can sing a song?" Pops asked as he finished writing what I said in the note pad.

"Yes sir, I can," Deon answered, then his phone rang "Sorry y'all, it's the forensic office, I have to take this call."

"Go ahead son," Mr. Fuller said. Deon got up out of his chair, pushed it in, then made his way outside.

"I think we should have a white marble type casket with green trimming to go with the white tux," Shy said.

"That's a good idea Shy. I'm glad I have y'all here because I wouldn't have thought of any of this on my own," Mr. Fuller said as he wrote down Shy's idea. He put the pencil down, sighed, and rubbed his forehead, "I wish I would have worked less and spent more time with my boy. I should know how my son would want his funeral to be and I don't because I was barely around him like I should have been. I was too focused on trying to keep myself busy dealing with the death of his mother instead of appreciating my time with him. Now I have no one." I watched as the tears began to run down his face.

"Pops it's okay, Rick understood, and he still loved you, that's all that matters," I could feel my eyes begin to water.

"I can't handle this," Shy exclaimed as she burst into tears. She got up from the table and ran outside. Mr. Fuller dried his eyes with a napkin that he had already been using, "I'm sorry baby girl, I shouldn't have gotten emotional around y'all, I should be the strong one."

"It's okay pops," I began to rub his back, "no need to hold back your emotions. Rick was your only son. But you're not alone, I'm here for you." Tears ran down both of our faces.

Deon walked back into the dining room. "I just saw Shy walk out crying, is everything good?"

"Yes, everything is fine. I think we've done enough for today. Maybe y'all can come back tomorrow evening? I'll cook a little something," Mr. Fuller answered.

"Yeah we'll come by then," I responded. Pops and I dried our eyes, stood up from the table and hugged. He walked over to Deon and hugged him. We made our way to the front door, I opened it and we saw Shy standing near the driver's side of my car. Pops stayed at the doorway, he waved bye to Shy and watched us as we got in our cars and left to head back to Deon's room.

Shy was quiet as she was drove. My mind began to wander as I looked out of the passenger side window.

I feel so bad for Pops. I can't believe that Rick, his only child, is really gone. Even though we didn't get much work done I'm glad that we got to see him, and I know that made him feel a little better. It's just all so overwhelming, the thought of Rick being in a casket and being laid to rest. And what Shy said about Lamar possibly being the one who did this to Rick, it's just not adding up. Hopefully after we all go to the police station for questioning it'll gets us closer to finding out who murdered Rick. But at this point my main focus is finding out what happened to his laptop. I'm sure whoever that was in Rick's room wearing all black has to have it, and I'm not going to stop until I find them.

I turned my head straight to look out of the front window to see that we were pulling up at Perry University. The time was about 4:30 PM. Either I was thinking for a long time or Shy drove really fast. She quickly found a parking spot in the main parking lot, parked and we got out and headed to Deon's dorm room. When we got inside his room, Deon walked in the kitchen area, Shy sat at the circle table and I sat down on the couch placing my bag on the side. Deon pulled out a bottle of alcohol. "Y'all want something to drink?"

"Give me a shot of whatever you got," Shy answered. I just sat there, staring off in space.

Deon snapped his fingers at me. "Ayo Riah do you want some of this liquor?"

I gathered myself, then looked at him, "Oh nah, I'm good D. Thank you though."

"What's on your mind Riah? Seems like you're thinking about something," Shy asked.

"I'm just trying to figure out what happened to Rick's laptop."

"Why is that so important to you?" Deon asked.

"Because Rick was talking to me on it. I remember the killer closing it after Rick fell to the ground, he could be the one who took it."

"Oool girl you might be on to something! Make sure you tell the officers that when you go to the station tomorrow," Shy said.

Deon walked over to her with a shot glass full of brown liquor and handed it to her. "What's tomorrow?" he asked.

Shy took her shot and placed the empty glass on the table, "Mariah gotta meet up with the officers for questioning and shit."

"Yeah, I witnessed so much that they feel my input would be beneficial. They're questioning Lamar, PJ, and Jordan as well," I chimed in.

Deon chuckled. "PJ's fat ass. Well iight just let me know how the questioning goes when you're done."

I nodded and gave him a small smile.

About 30-45 minutes went by, I was still sitting on the couch thinking to myself and looking through Rick's phone while Shy and Deon were still taking shots at the table.

"Damn Mariah, you need to loosen up. Don't have me and Shy

turning up on our own," Deon said in a slurred voice. I put Rick's phone back in my hoody pocket, "How can I loosen up and my boyfriend just died," I said with attitude, "y'all sitting here partying it up like y'all don't even care."

"Mariah it's not like that, you know we care, but everybody handles things differently," Shy said. Deon got up from the table, grabbed a shot glass, poured some liquor, and then made his way to me.

"Here man just take a shot," he said, holding the glass out for me to grab.

I turned my head away and held my hand up. "No, I don't want one."

"Just take one man," Deon said, raising his voice.

"I said no!" I shouted in response.

"Here!" He yelled.

I turned back to face him and knocked the full shot glass out of his hand. "I said no! Now don't ask me anymore."

Deon started breathing heavily. "Aye bruh you tripping."

I was about to say something else, but I suddenly felt like I was going to throw up. I got up from the couch, holding my stomach and covering my mouth and ran to the trash can.

"Whoa Riah you good?" Shy jumped up out of her chair and came over to me. She rubbed my back then turned to Deon and said, "Y'all lets calm down man."

I finished vomiting, my stomach empty, and wiped the corners of my mouth. I stood up and looked at my friends. "I'm just stressed. I think I'm just going to stay at my parents' house tonight."

Deon came over to me and grabbed my arm. "Wait Riah I'm sorry, I didn't mean to upset you. I'm hurting too you know."

"Yeah Riah you don't have to leave. We can have a chill night with no drinking if that's what you want," Shy chimed in.

"Yeah man, I'll chill," Deon added.

"Okay, I'll stay," I said as I walked back to the couch, "But I'm not in the mood for conversation." I sat down and pulled Rick's phone back out of my hoody pocket. They sat back down at their seats at the table. Shy's phone rang. "Ugh this boy is so aggravating," she said after checking the caller id.

"Who is that, boyfriend number 10?" Deon asked.

"No, it's actually boyfriend number nine," She responded, showing Deon her phone screen.

Deon shook his head. "The fact that you actually have it saved as that is ridiculous."

Shy laughed a little, "Man look I get it how I live. Anyways I'm gone call him back because I think I need me an appointment tonight."

"What do you mean an appointment?"

"What I just said, an appointment."

"Wow, you're disgusting."

"I need to go take me a shower before I call him back telling him to pull up." Shy got up out of her chair. She mushed Deon in the head as she passed him then walked over to me. "Give me a hug Mariah even though you're upset with me." She stood in front of me with her arms extended for a hug.

I looked up from the phone and leaned up to give her a side hug. "Later."

"I love you Mariah," she said with a disappointed look on her face. Shy walked back past Deon and said, "Bye Deon. I'll see y'all tomorrow," as she made her way out of the door.

Deon stood up, walked to the door and locked it. He turned to me, "You got that same expression on your face from when we were younger, and you would get upset with me."

I looked at him then looked back down at Rick's phone, "Shut up Deon."

"What? I'm just saying some things never change." He must have noticed that the phone I had wasn't mine because then he asked, "Did you get a new phone?"

I was hesitant to answer at first because I didn't want him to know that I had Rick's phone. I finally spoke up and said, "Yeah, I wanted to match Rick's."

"Oh, that's cute."

We were silent for a few seconds before he asked, "You want to sleep with me tonight? You know like when we were kids?"

I looked back up from the phone at him, "Rick stop, we're not kids anymore."

He stood there looking at me with his mouth wide opened then said, "Deon..."

"What?" I asked.

"You called me Rick."

I looked at him with a blank expression, "I'm sorry, it's been a long day. I think I need to take a quick walk around campus to clear my mind."

He said "okay" as he nodded and opened the door for me as I walked past him to go outside.

I walked all around the campus from the Student Union, to the Sports Arena, and behind several different buildings. Everywhere I walked I saw something that reminded me of Rick, it brought back memories of us being together. I made my way to the nature walk which was a special place for me. Rick and I spent a good amount of time walking through there, looking to see if we would see any animals. There's this one bench that we would always sit on, by the pond that was beside the nature trail. I walked over to it and sat down, looking up at the sky. I could kind of see Rick's face in some of the clouds, made me smile a lot. I soon stood from the bench, I bent down and grabbed some stones and started skipping them across the pond. I saw his face again through the ripples of the water. I took that as his way of showing me that he's always going to be with me, wherever I go. Seeing his face while on the walk really helped me clear my mind.

After about an hour of walking around the campus I decided to head back to Deon's room. I definitely wanted to apologize to him and Shy for acting the way I did earlier. When I made it to Deon's dorm room the front door was unlocked so I walked in and called his name, but he didn't respond. I walked to his room door but it was closed and locked. I knocked a couple of times, but I still didn't get a response, so I assumed he wasn't there. I walked back to the front room, sat on the couch, pulled out my phone and called Shy.

She answered after a few rings. "Hey girl what's up," she whispered.

"Girl why are you whispering?"

"I'm kind of in the middle of something but I'll be done in like five minutes."

"Okay whatever. Never mind, I'll talk to you later." I ended the call and stared at the ceiling trying to figure out what to do since Shy was busy and Deon wasn't here. I figured I would just take a long shower to pass time then I could lay down afterwards. I looked to the side of the couch where my duffle bag was. I reached into it, grabbed my purple pajamas and then headed to the bathroom to shower.

I stayed in the shower about 30 minutes, that's about when the water started getting cold, and as I was getting ready to walk out of the bathroom I bumped into Deon.

"I'm sorry," I said to him as I stood there with my dirty clothes in my hand.

"It's cool, my bad," he looked at the clothes in my hand, "You need a bag for those?"

"Yes please."

He walked to the kitchen, pulled a plastic bag out of a drawer, and walked back over to me, "Here you go," he said, handing me the bag. I took the bag, told him thanks, and walked back to the living room. I put the bag of dirty clothes in my duffle bag and flopped down on the couch.

"You're not still mad, are you?" Deon yelled from his room.

"No, I'm not mad anymore...I just have a lot on my mind right now."

"I feel you. Just don't think I don't care, because I do."

"I know you do," I said. Then I stretched out on the couch.

Deon came into the front room, "Nah Riah, you take the bed I'll take the sofa."

"It's fine, I'm already here anyways."

"Well at least let me get you a blanket and a pillow."

"Okay." Deon walked back to his room then came back with a blanket and pillow in hand and walked over to give it to me.

"Here you go," He said holding the pillow and blanket out to me.

I leaned up to grab the stuff, "Thanks, think I'm going to call it a night."

He pulled his phone out of his pocket and checked the time, "This early?"

"Yeah didn't get any sleep last night after everything happened."

"Alright, well I guess I'll see you when you wake up."

"Okay good night."

"Good night," he said as he walked over to cut the room light off then walked to his room. I laid back down, spreading the cover on me and laying my head on the pillow. Once I got comfortable, I grabbed the heart charm on my necklace, brought it to my mouth and kissed it. "I love you Rick," I said as my eyes closed shut.

WHAT'S REALLY GOING ON

I woke up that next morning a little after 8:30 to my phone ringing loudly. I felt around for it, my eyes still closed. I finally found it and opened one of my eyes to see who it was calling and saw that it was Lamar.

"Hello," I answered, my voice rough.

"Hey Mariah, sorry about waking you up, just wanted to see what time you were going to be heading to the police station today?"

I pulled the phone from my ear to check the time, put it back to my ear and said, "I'll probably head up there about 11 so I can get it out of the way. What about y'all?"

"We're at practice right now, it'll be over at 10 o'clock. PJ was saying we should go after practice so like one o'clock I guess," I heard some shuffling on the other end of the call, "stop fat boy I'm on the phone with Mariah." I heard PJ in the background say, "Let me talk to her."

"No man move, we are trying to handle business." Lamar snapped back. I guess PJ ended up getting the phone from Lamar. "Sissssss," he said from the other end.

I chuckled, "Good morning PJ, how are you?"

"I'm good what about you?"

"I'm doing better than yesterday," I said as Deon walked out of his room, wearing basketball shorts, socks, and slides, and came into the front room, "I'll chat with you later though PJ."

"Alright, later."

I hung up and put my phone on the arm of the couch.

"Good morning," Deon said as he came and sat by me, "what PJ was talking about?"

"Nothing really, he was just checking on me and was seeing what time I was going to the station."

"Cool, so what time are you going?"

"I told them about eleven but I will probably just go when they get out of practice and settled which will be about one o'clock or so. Let me call Officer Anderson now before it get too late." I leaned up over the arm of the couch to grab Officer Anderson's card out of the bag that my dirty clothes were in. I grabbed the card then grabbed my phone to make the call.

"Alright, well what do you want to eat for breakfast? I'm going to cook," Deon asked.

"It doesn't matter to me."

Officer Anderson didn't answer so I left him a voicemail informing him on what time the boys and I were going to come to the station for questioning. After I hung up the phone there was a loud bang at the front door. Deon got up from the couch and walked to the door and asked, "Who is it?"

The person on the other side didn't say anything so Deon peeped through the peep hole.

"They covering the hole," he said. He opened the door and Shy barged in wearing a black sweatshirt, olive green leggings, and slides.

"Good morning niggas! What are we eating for breakfast?" she yelled. She looked at Deon and put her hand over her mouth, "Ewww Deon where is your shirt?"

"In my room man," he replied.

"You need to put that shit on."

Deon sucked his teeth, laughed and said, "Here your ass go," then he closed the front door.

I sighed in relief and laid back down on the couch, "Dammit Shy, you scared me."

"My bad girl," she walked over to me and bent down to give me a hug, "How are you?"

I leaned up to give her a hug, "I'm good."

She jumped back before we completed the hug, covered her nose and said, "Damn Mariah did you eat ass before you went to bed?"

Deon laughed, "Chill Shy she just really woke up."

I laughed, covered my mouth. I grabbed my toothbrush and toothpaste from my duffel and ran to the bathroom sink to go brush my teeth, "Shyyyy leave me alone," I yelled as I turned the water on.

She laughed and said, "Don't be so sensitive Riah."

"Shut up," I yelled.

"So, about breakfast?" I heard Shy ask Deon.

"What y'all want me to cook?" + Deon asked back.

"You about to cook?"

"Yeah nigga."

Shy leaned off of the counter and walked back to the couch and sat down then said, "I'll pass."

I finished brushing my teeth and headed back in the front room. I saw Shy sitting down on the couch and Deon leaning against the kitchen counter.

"Shy don't do D like that."

"Girl remember he burnt that food that one time. Nope, I am straight."

I chuckled, "Oh yea I remember that, that was funny."

"Come on y'all, that was when I was just getting in the groove of cooking. That was the first and only time I burned food," Deon said from the kitchen.

"Yeah yeah I don't believe you," Shy said.

"Well don't eat then," he laughed, "What you want Mariah?"

"Whatever you cook is fine with me D."

"Cool, so I'm going to do pancakes, eggs, and bacon." He started getting the stuff he needed to cook with.

"That'll work."

"Yeah that'll work." Shy added.

Deon stopped what he was doing and looked at Shy, "Oh now you want some huh?"

"I really just want some bacon," she replied.

He laughed, shook his head then started back prepping the food. "I got y'all, it shouldn't take too long."

Deon pulled eggs and bacon out of the refrigerator, grabbed the pancake mix from the top of the fridge, then grabbed two mixing bowls out of the cabinets. I walked over to the couch to join Shy. Shy grabbed the remote to the TV, turned it on and started flipping through the channels.

"Cartoons it is," she said as she stopped the TV on cartoons.

"Ain't nothing wrong with cartoons," I said.

"True. What time were you going to go to the police station?"

"I was going to go at eleven but I'm going to wait until one when PJ, Jordan, and Lamar get settled from practice."

"Oh, you already talked to them?"

"Yes, Lamar called me this morning," I laughed, "then PJ took the phone from him. That boy silly."

"Oh ok," she sucked her teeth, "girl why the fuck PJ's ass text me last night?"

I chuckled, "For real, what did he say?"

"Yes girl, nigga gone ask me what I was on."

"What you said?"

"Some dick!"

I burst out laughing, "You said that for real?"

"Yes, 'cause it was the truth."

I shook my head while still laughing a little, "GIRL!!! Shy I swear you is crae crae."

"Girl nobody got time for Percival Jenkins' big ass."

"The fact that his mama named him that though."

"Right?? All those boy names out there that start with a 'P' and she chose Percival." Shy and I both started laughing and then my phone rang. I grabbed it and saw that it was my dad calling so I answered.

"Hey daddy."

"Hey baby girl, how are you?"

"I'm good, sitting with Shy and Deon in his room."

"Oh okay, tell them both I said hello." I put the phone down from my ear and told them my dad said hello. They both said spoke, then I put the phone back to my ear, "They said hey daddy."

"Alright, so what are you doing today?" my daddy asked.

"I'm supposed to go to the police station at one o'clock to tell them what all I saw Friday night."

"So, they gone ask you some questions and stuff?"

"Yes sir."

"Oh okay, why at one o'clock though?"

"Well one o'clock is when Rick's roommates are available to go up there, so we can get it out the way at the same time."

"Well that's alright. Make sure you let me know what they say."

"Yes sir."

"I just got finished getting dressed."

"Where's mom?"

"Oh, she in the bathroom finishing her hair so we can head on to church."

"Oh, it is Sunday. Well I'll let you go, I'll call y'all when I leave the station. Hopefully y'all are out of church by then, you know Pastor Lewis long winded." I laughed. My dad laughed then said, "Yes Lord he is. We'll talk later baby girl, I love you."

"Okay I love you too."

"Later."

"Later." I hung up the phone and started watching the TV.

"Damn Chef Boyardee! Is the food ready yet?" Shy yelled in the direction of the kitchen.

"Almost man, I got about two more pancakes to make."

"Hopefully me and Riah don't die of starvation by then."

"Your ass always talking shit."

"That's what I do," she said, smiling real big.

"Shy do you want to go the police station with me?" I asked.

She looked at me, "That's cool. Boyfriend number six was supposed to take me to brunch at one but I'll just tell him I'll just catch him another time."

"Shy do you really have ten boyfriends?"

"I mean of course they not all my boyfriends, I just call them that.

And I only have sex with two of them."

"I was about to say girl," I chuckled.

Shy laughed, "You know I got to have my options girl."

"Right."

"Alright ladies, breakfast is ready. Riah, want me to fix your plate?" Deon asked from the kitchen

"Yeah that's fine."

"Damn am I invisible or some shit?" Shy said, waving her hands in front of her face.

Deon sighed, laughed, then asked, "Would you like for me to fix your plate Shy?"

"Oh my gosh sure Deon, you're the best," she answered sarcastically.

"You get on my nerves girl," he laughed, "do you want pancakes and eggs too?"

"Yes, one pancake and a little bit of eggs."

"I got you," he said, then started fixing our plates. Once he finished fixing the plates he walked over to Shy and I and handed them to us, "What y'all want to drink?"

"Water for me," I answered.

"You got orange juice?" Shy asked.

"Should, let me check though." He walked to the fridge, opened it then said, "Yeah it's some in here."

"That's what I want."

Deon pulled the orange juice out of the fridge along with a bottle of water and sat them both on the counter. He opened the cabinet to grab a cup, poured the orange juice in the cup. He put the carton back in the fridge, then brought us our drinks. He went back to the kitchen to fix his plate then sat at the table to eat.

"Y'all niggas really sitting here watching cartoons," Deon said.

"Ain't nothing on TV this early in the morning except church services."

"Y'all asses need some Jesus in ya lives."

"You know what you need Deon?" Shy asked.

"What?"

"To shut the fuck up," she said then laughed.

I laughed, "I saw that coming."

Deon started laughing with me and Shy, "I should have too, hell."

"Should've could've would've but you didn't," said Shy.

"Whatever bald head," Deon said.

"Who bald head?"

Deon laughed then said, "You, nigga."

"Boy ain't," Shy ran one hand through her long weave, "I know you see these inches."

Deon laughed again, "That ain't even yours."

"I bought it with my money and put it in, so it is mine," Shy said as she flicked him off.

I laughed, "I know that's right Shy."

"Girl, Deon better act like he know."

"Yeah yeah," he said.

"Anyways, Mariah when are you going back to Livingston," Shy asked.

"After Thanksgiving break."

"What about your job?"

"Girl you know I'm off every weekend anyways so I told my boss about what happened and she gave me one week off plus I already had the week of thanksgiving off."

"Oooh. Okay cool then."

"Yup," I looked at Deon and asked, "so what you got planned today D?"

"Shit I'm supposed to get up with my study group at the library around like two. Got a test Tuesday and Thursday."

"Deon, even though I be going off on you a lot, I just want you to know I am very proud of you, your major is the hardest out of all of ours and you're keeping your grades up so well," Shy said.

"Damn Shy, you're being nice to me? I appreciate it though," Deon said as he stood from his chair and walked up to Shy to try to give her a hug. She leaned away from his hug.

"Alright now you doing too much. Can't never be nice to niggas."

"Shy stop it," I laughed.

"It's alright, I know Shy love me," Deon said as he walked back to the table.

"Yeah I love you man. But anyways, I'm about to go finish Chelsea's hair, I was supposed to finish it days ago," Shy said as she got up and took her dishes to the sink. She looked at me from the sink and said, "I'll be back in time enough for us to go to the station together."

"Okay cool see you then."

She walked to the front door, opened it, stopped, then yelled, "See yaaaaa," then walked out, closing the door behind her.

That girl Shy Monroe is one of a kind man.

I got up from the couch and walked to the sink to start washing the dirty dishes. I cut the water on and put dish liquid in the sink on the side where I placed the dishes.

"Deon?"

"Yo?" he replied then got up and brought his dirty dishes to the sink.

"Who's Chelsea?" I asked as I grabbed the dirty dishes out of his hand and placed them in the water.

"Some big girl Shy be with now," he replied then walked over to the couch and sat down.

I laughed, "Wow."

"What?"

"That must be the girl Rick was talking about."

"Yeah, shit, probably."

"Mm yeah," I said after I let the water out of the sink. "I'm about to take a shower," I said drying my hands off with a towel on the counter.

"Iight cool."

I walked over to the side of the couch where my bag was to grab some clean clothes out of it then headed to the shower.

I didn't take a long shower like I did the night before because I didn't want to use all of the hot water before Deon took his shower. I walked out of the bathroom wearing a long sleeve pow-der blue polo shirt, blue jeans, white tennis shoes, and a scarf around my neck. I took my pajamas and put them in my bag. I walked to the front door and cracked it. I turned to Deon, who was still sitting on the couch watching TV, "I'm going to go sit at the gazebo right there, it looks nice out."

"Alright, make sure you are back by the time Shy gets here."

"Yes dad," I said sarcastically. We both laughed. I left the room, closing the door behind me, and walked to the gazebo that was right outside of Deon's building.

I sat down at the bench, watching the people walk by. I noticed Lamar standing outside of a building, still wearing his practice clothes, with three guys, all of them wearing all black. He turned in my direction and I waved at him but he didn't see me, so I decided to walk over to where he was. When I got closer to him he was facing the three guys, so I tapped him on the shoulder, "Hey Lamar."

He jumped a little then turned around, "Oh shit what's good Riah."

I was about to answer him but one of the guys, a tall light-skinned guy with dreads, cut me off, "Damn Lamar this how you handle business cuz?"

"Yeah man this what we doing now?" one of the other guys, a shorter bald dude, asked.

"Naw it's not like that, this my home girl." Lamar answered.

"You look familiar, you go here?" The third guy asked, staring me in my face. He had long messy dreads.

"No, my boyfriend did though," I responded.

"Did? What's his name?" The bald guy asked.

"Rick Fuller," I said.

"Rick was yo nigga?" the dread-head asked. He looked at Lamar and pointed at me, "Naw bro she gotta go."

"Excuse me?" I said, confused.

"Aye Avery chill," Lamar said to the dread-head. Lamar looked at me, "Can you just go? I'll holla at you later."

I looked at Avery, who was standing there with a smirk on his face, then looked back at Lamar and just walked off back to the gazebo.

I sat at the table in the center of the gazebo, facing Deon's building. I looked over my shoulder back in the direction where Lamar, Avery and the two guys were. I shook my head and turned back around and saw Deon walking towards me wearing a black pull over, gray sweat pants, and black tennis shoes. He had his book bag on and a textbook in his hand.

"Ayo Riah I just wanted to let you know I'm going to meet with my study group early and I left the front door unlocked for you."

"Okay I'll see you later."

"Alright, later," he said, then walked off in the direction of the library.

I didn't stay outside too much longer after Deon walked off because it got a little windy and I wanted to try to catch a nap before Shy came. I got up and walked back to Deon's room. Once I got inside I locked the front door, laid on the couch and fell straight to sleep. While I was asleep, I dreamt that Rick and I were on face-time and we were wearing the same clothes we had on the night he was murdered. I was staring at him while he was sitting in his desk chair crying.

"Babe what's wrong?" I asked.

"He betrayed me," he said, still crying.

"Who betrayed you?"

"He betrayed me. He betrayed me. He betrayed me. He be…" A figure, dressed in all black just like the murderer from that night, appeared behind Rick, stabbing him

"Riiiiiick!" I screamed as he fell to the floor.

I woke up with sweat on my forehead, my heart racing. I grabbed my phone to see what time it was and saw that I had been asleep for an hour. I went to go dial Shy's number but then there was a knock on the front door. I just sat there and looked at it for a minute before moving, and then there was another knock but this time I heard Shy say my name as she knocked again. I jumped up quickly and walked over to the door to open it for her. She was wearing a gray thermal shirt, gray leggings, and gray and white tennis shoes.

"Hey girl, sorry I'm a little late. Are you okay?" She asked me with a concerned look on her face.

"Yeah," I said as I wiped sweat off my forehead, "I had a bad dream

Anthony Taylor

that's all, I'm good now though. Are you ready?"

"Oh, okay just checking. I'm ready if you ready though."

I walked out of Deon's room, closing the door behind me, and we headed toward the parking lot to my car. I got in the driver's seat, Shy got on the passenger side, I started the car and pulled out of the lot.

"So, girl some weird shit happened earlier today after you left."

"With who?" Shy asked while looking at me.

"With Lamar," I glanced over and saw Shy's confused expression.

"What happened?"

I told Shy everything that happened outside with Lamar, Avery, and I. "Girl it was crazy."

Shy banged on the dashboard, "Bitch I told you! I knew it, he did it! He fucking did it!"

I shook my head, "I don't want to believe that, but everything you've said is adding up at this point. I just don't understand why he would do that to Rick though."

"It's always the ones you least expect. Wait, did you say it was Avery he was talking to that started tripping?"

"Yes, and there was two other boys, but they didn't trip like that. It was only the Avery dude that did. Why what's up?" I glanced over to see that Shy had turned to look out the window.

"Oh, it's nothing," she said.

I didn't say anything after that and we were silent for the rest of the drive. When we got to the police station, I parked the car and we got out. I locked the doors and we walked towards the station's entrance. PJ, Jordan and Lamar were walking up at the same time.

"What's up y'all," PJ said to Shy and I.

Jordan waved. Lamar didn't say anything.

64

"Hey," I said dryly, not making eye contact.

"Hey PJ, hey Jordan," Shy said. She looked at Lamar and rolled her eyes. Shy and I walked into the station.

"Damn, wassup with them?" Jordan asked.

"I don't know, maybe they're stressed out about this questioning shit," PJ responded.

Lamar took a deep breath and walked into the police station. PJ and Jordan followed him in, exchanging confused looks. After we all got inside of the station, we were split up and sent into different interrogation rooms. Shy was left to wait for us in the lobby. This was my first interrogation, so I didn't know what to expect. The only knowledge I really had about how an interrogation was ran was from watching First 48 on TV. I figured since it was a group of us we would be asked similar questions or different ones based off the answers that we gave. I didn't know, I was just ready to get the shit over with so I could go on about my day.

Officer Anderson finally came into the room where I was and sat across from me at the table. He placed a note pad on the table and pulled out a pen as he sat down.

Officer Anderson: So let's get right to it. What's your relation to the victim?

Me: Rick, I mean Richard, was my boyfriend since our freshman year of high school. We also grew up together. We started off as friends and it eventually developed into something more after his mom passed.

Officer Anderson: What's your relation to the victim?

Jordan: We were on the basketball team together since last year and we've been roommates since the beginning of this semester.

Officer Anderson: What is your relation to the victim?

PJ: He was my teammate on the basketball team and we've been roommates since last year. It was me, him, and one of his friends named Deon.

Officer Anderson: What is your relation to the victim?

Lamar: He was my teammate and we roomed together. We were pretty tight.

Officer Anderson: What were you doing this past Friday night around the time the incident occurred?

Me: I was at school, Livingston University, doing laundry and waiting for Rick to facetime me so we could talk. Being that he was so busy the whole week we didn't really have a chance to talk to each other.

Officer Anderson: What were you doing this past Friday night around the time the incident occurred?

Jordan: Me, PJ and Lamar was getting ready to head out to club Lava and before we left we were trying to convince Rick to come out with us but he wouldn't, he said he had to talk to Mariah that night.

Officer Anderson: What were you doing this past Friday night around the time the incident occurred?

PJ: Me and the boys was getting ready to go out, we wanted Rick to come with us but he didn't want to so we left him at the room. Me and Jordan road together while Lamar drove separately.

Officer Anderson: What were you doing this past Friday night around the time the incident occurred?

Lamar: It was a boy's night out so we went to club lava. Only me, PJ and Jordan went though. I drove my own car to the club and left Lava before them though because I had other plans.

Officer Anderson: Other plans like what?

Lamar: I do have other friends, so I wanted to hang out with them that night too so that's what I did.

Officer Anderson: Do you know of anyone Fuller may have had

issues with?

Me: When we were younger, like freshman year of high school, Rick was heavy in the streets but, when he came to college he left that life behind him so I don't know of anyone he could have any problems with or vice versa.

Officer Anderson: What do you mean heavy in the streets?

Me: Well what do you think, he was a young black male who lost his mother to cancer during an important time in his life where he needed his mother. It's self-explanatory, really.

Officer Anderson: Do you know of anyone Fuller may have had issues with?

Jordan: The only person I can really think of is one of our teammates, Avery Singleton.

Officer Anderson: Do you know of anyone Fuller may have had issues with?

PJ: Bitch ass Avery Singleton.

Officer Anderson: Do you know of anyone Fuller may have had issues with?

Lamar: Naw I can't think of anyone he had issues with.

Officer Anderson: What caused the turmoil between Singleton and Fuller?

Jordan: Once Rick made the team, Avery wasn't getting as much play time as he was used to. He was on the team before we got there but the better player, which was Rick, took his spot. So I guess you could say jealousy.

Officer Anderson: What caused the turmoil between Singleton and Fuller?

PJ: Jealousy man, my boy Rick was a beast on the court, and if we being completely honest, Rick was the team. Avery didn't like that and on top of that he wasn't getting any play time like that.

Officer Anderson: Tell me what you know about Fuller's death.

Me: Well, like I said we were on FaceTime on our Mac-books and while we were talking I saw someone dressed in all black and a skully or something over their face. I told Rick about it but he said it was probably just one of his roommates' flings, Lacy. Then we heard pots and pans from the kitchen falling over so he went to go check on the noise and when he came back into the room he was bleeding, from stab wounds it seemed like. He told me that he loved me and for me to call the police, then he fell to the ground.

Officer Anderson: Tell me what you know about Fullers death.

Jordan: I didn't witness the actual murder, but me and PJ was on our way back to the room and saw police cars everywhere. We asked what happened and one of the officers told us that Rick was murdered from stab wounds.

Officer Anderson: Tell me what you know about Fullers death.

PJ: Man after me and Jordan got back from Lava, police cars was everywhere, and that's when we found out somebody killed Rick. We couldn't believe our dawg was gone.

Officer Anderson: Tell me what you know about Fullers death.

Lamar: I wasn't on campus when it happened. Jordan called me and told me what went down, so I rushed back on campus from where I was and when I got to the room I found out it was true. Shit crazy man.

Officer Anderson: Who is Lacy?

Jordan: Aw man that's PJ ole lady.

Officer Anderson: Who is Lacy?

PJ: That's a girl I mess with here and there, but aye what she gotta do with this?

Officer Anderson: I ask the questions around here, Jenkins.

PJ: Whatever you say, Anderson.

Officer Anderson: Do you know where she was the night of the incident?

PJ: Before we left for the club she said she might stop by the room and wait for me there, but when I called her telling her I was on my way back she told me she was tired and had to work the next morning so she was at her room not mine.

Officer Anderson: Who is Lacy?

Lamar: That's a female PJ messes with on a regular. Always like to pop up at the room even when PJ not there. Chick crazy.

Officer Anderson: Alright that's all the questions I have for you. I appreciate you coming in to clarify some things and once again I am sorry for your loss. We will keep you updated on the progress of this investigation. What we have discussed in here today is confidential information and should not be shared with anyone.

"Thank you," I got out of my chair and walked to the door, Officer Anderson stood there holding it open for me. I walked out of the room and made my way back to the front where Shy was. Anderson walked into the room that I saw Jordan go into earlier. When I got to the front I picked up my cellphone from the person at the front desk; we had to leave them up there, and I went and sat by Shy to wait on everybody else.

Officer Anderson: Alright that's all the questions I have for you. I appreciate you coming in to clarify some things and once again I am sorry for your loss. We will keep you updated on the progress of this investigation. What we have discussed in here today is confidential information and should not be shared with anyone.

Jordan: Yes sir thank you.

Not even 20 minutes after I was finished with my session Jordan walked out of his room and came and stood by me and Shy. We all had looks on our faces like we wanted to talk about what happened during the interrogations but we couldn't since we were still inside the station.

Officer Anderson: Alright that's all the questions I have for you. I appreciate you coming in to clarify some things and once again I am sorry for your loss. We will keep you updated on the progress of this investigation. What we have discussed in here today is confidential information and should not be shared with anyone.

PJ: 'Preciate it.

Another 20 minutes passed and PJ walked up to where we were and was about to start talking, but we all shook our heads to let him know not to say anything while we were still inside.

Lamar's session got lengthy, so Jordan asked if we all wanted to go outside and talk until Lamar got finished. We all agreed and Shy and I made our way outside while PJ and Jordan grabbed their cellphones from the person at the front desk. They grabbed their phones then came outside to where Shy and I were standing. We all talked about the questions that Officer Anderson asked us, although he told us not to discuss it with anyone.

Lamar: So is that all your questions?

Officer Anderson: Not quite, I have one more question for you. Who is Avery Singleton?

Lamar: He's one of our teammates on the basketball team, and I guess you can say he's a friend of mine also.

Officer Anderson: You guess he's a friend?

Lamar: I mean, yeah. We hang out here and there, that's about it though.

Officer Anderson: Alright that's all I have for you. We'll be in touch.

In the middle of us talking Lamar finally came outside, after about 30 minutes of talking with Anderson. He saw where we were standing and walked over to us.

"Yo Mariah can I talk to you," he asked, looking at me.

"What do you want to talk to her about?" Shy interjected, moving to stand in front of me.

"Shy why you always got an attitude? This don't concern you, I'm trying to talk to my sis."

"Am I really your sis? 'Cause how you acted earlier says differently," I said as I moved from behind Shy.

Lamar stood there quietly, nodding his head at me and Shy then said, "Iight bet." He turned to look at PJ, "Open the car up P, I ain't got time for this shit man."

PJ unlocked his car and Lamar walked over to it and got in the back seat.

"What happened earlier," Jordan asked as he moved in closer to me and Shy.

"What happened was Lamar was acting real shady and we don't like it," Shy answered before I could.

"Shady like how," PJ asked as he came in closer.

"Yeah what happened," Jordan asked.

"I walked up on him talking with three guys and one of them told me I had to leave because Rick was my boyfriend," I finally answered.

"Damn that's fucked up," Jordan said, shaking his head, "Do you know any of the guys' names?"

"I know one of the guys' name was Avery."

"Avery!" PJ responded angrily.

"Yo what the fuck is Lamar on?" Jordan said then looked at PJ, "Let's ride PJ." Jordan looked back at me, "Sis we will holla at you later." He hugged then PJ gave me a hug too. They both told Shy bye then got in their car and headed to campus. I noticed Shy was standing off to the side quiet and I looked at her suspiciously.

"What's up Shy, are you okay," I asked.

"Yeah I'm good let's just go," she responded before heading to the driver side of my car. She got in and started the engine. I stood there for a minute staring at her through the windows of the car before finally walking over to the passenger side to get in.

"Shy, you are my best friend and you know I know when something is up with you right?"

"I know but I promise nothing is up, I'm good," she said with a fake smile on her face. I didn't believe at all that she was good but I let her have it. We sat in silence for a while on the way back to campus. Shy's phone started ringing from her purse which was on the floor between my feet.

"Riah can you get that for me," she asked, pointing at her purse on the floor. I reached down and grabbed her phone out of the purse and answered it without looking to see who it was.

"Hello," I said while I waited for the facetime call to connect. When the call finally connected I was shocked to see Avery's face pop up on the phone screen. He was just as shocked to see me as I was to see him.

"Hello," he exclaimed.

I turned the phone away from me and pointed it in the direction of Shy.

"Mariah who is it," Shy asked. She quickly glanced at her phone and saw that it was Avery on the phone, "Umm hey Avery let me hit you back a little later."

"Iight," he said then ended the call.

I put Shy's phone back in her purse, looked at her and asked, "Shy what is really going on?"

"Look Riah I don't want you to judge me okay," she said trying not to make eye contact with me.

"Judge you?"

"Yes, Riah judge me. I knew if you found out I was fucking with a guy that everyone knew Rick was beefing with you would judge me."

"I didn't even know Rick was beefing with anyone. Why didn't anyone tell me anything? This could be the muthafucka who killed my damn boyfriend, a close friend of yours, and nobody's saying nothing!" I said furiously.

Shy didn't say anything and continued to just stare at the road as she drove. I was about to say something else but then my phone rung. I pulled it out of my pocket, saw it was my dad and I answered.

"Hey daddy."

"Hey sweetie, is the questioning over?"

"Yes sir the questioning is over. I'm heading back to campus now."

"Okay good, your mom and I are home from church. I think she is about to cook dinner."

"Okay I will be there shortly."

"Sounds good baby girl, love you."

"Love you too daddy."

"Later."

"Later."

I hung up the phone. For the rest of the drive back to campus, Shy and I were quiet. I had nothing to say to her honestly, so I just stared out the window. But I later heard from PJ and Jordan that their ride home was much livelier.

Jordan was driving them back to campus, with PJ in the passenger seat and Lamar in the back, texting on his phone. The car was quiet except for the sound of Lamar's typing.

"Fuck this quiet shit," PJ exclaimed suddenly. He turned in his seat to look at Lamar, "What's up with you nigga?"

Lamar looked up from his phone, unbothered by PJ's outburst. "Fuck is you talking 'bout bruh?"

"I'm talking 'bout the fact that you been hanging with the enemy, that's real shady."

Lamar sighed, "So I'm guessing Mariah told y'all she saw me talking to Avery earlier."

"Why you say that like it's nothing," Jordan said, "don't you think your boys should be the first ones to know that you decided to be friends with someone we don't fuck with like that?"

"We all knew Avery had some pressure with Rick and for you to be cool with him is messed up, especially now since Rick is gone," PJ said. He faced forward in his seat, "I think Avery had something to do with Rick's murder, and maybe you did too."

"Really P," Lamar said incredulously, "you think I would do something like that?"

PJ didn't say anything. Lamar leaned forward in his seat and looks at Jordan, "So you think that too J?"

"I don't know man," Jordan shrugged, "shit just not adding up. I don't know what to think right now."

Lamar leaned back into his seat and looked back and forth between PJ and Jordan.

"Bet. Well if y'all think that low of me then fuck y'all!"

"Fuck us?" PJ shouted, turning back around to face Lamar, "Nah nigga fuck you! Ole snake ass nigga!"

Lamar unbuckled his seatbelt, leaning towards PJ, "PJ you talking like you wanna do something, what's up nigga?"

PJ grabbed Lamar by his collar and the two started to tussle. Jordan did his best to steer the car with his left hand while he tried to break up the fight with his right.

"Aye y'all chill man, I'm trying to drive," Jordan yelled.

PJ hit Lamar in his mouth, busting his lip, before turning back around and sitting in his seat. Lamar fell back into the back seat and held his bleeding lip.

"Stop the car and let me out! I'll walk the rest of the way to campus," Lamar said in a muffled voice.

"Nah, we almost there. Just chill," Jordan responded.

"Nah, let me out. I can't be in the car with his fat ass no longer," Lamar replied, pulling on the door handle.

"Well get yo snake ass out then," PJ said.

Jordan pulled the car over and unlocked the doors. Lamar got out and slammed the door behind him and started walking towards the campus. Jordan pulled off and started snickering.

"Hell you laughing at J," PJ asked.

"Man yo big ass almost made me crash with all that jiggling you did to get Lamar."

PJ sucked his teeth, "Man whatever, I'm hungry, pull up to the caf."

PJ and Jordan continued back to campus and went to the cafeteria to eat when they got there. By this time, Shy and I were pulling into the campus parking lot close to where her room was.

SUPPORT ME

"Riah, I..." Shy started to say while looking at me, but before she finished her statement I cut her off, "I really don't want to hear it Shy. I am about to go to my parents' house. I'll catch up with you later." She looked at me with a sad expression on her face before she finally got out of the driver's seat and started walking to her room. I got into the driver's seat then pulled out of the parking lot headed to my parents' house.

My thoughts ran a mile a minute while I was driving, and I was starting to get a little headache. I just couldn't believe Shy was acting like that; she is supposed to be my best friend but couldn't even tell me what's really going on. First Lamar, now Shy and it's all based around this Avery dude. I hoped that my parents would've given me some guidance, or at least a peace of mind, but they didn't really make things better either.

Ten minutes had passed by as I pulled up to my parents' house. I unlocked the door, walked inside and said, "Hello?" as I closed the door behind me.

"Hey Riah baby I'm here in the kitchen," my mom yelled out. I walked down the hallway to the kitchen and saw her standing at the stove with her white floral dress on that she wore to church. I walked up behind her, "Hey ma," I said as I hugged her.

"Hey sweetie, how are you?"

I sighed, "The best I can be honestly." I walked over to the kitchen table and sat down.

"I know it's hard baby, but with God on your side, you are going to get through this."

"Yes ma'am, how was church?"

"It was good, Pastor Lewis asked about you."

"I have to make sure I see him next Sunday since I didn't make it to church this morning."

"Hey baby girl," my dad said as he walked in the kitchen still wearing what he wore to church as well. He came up to me and gave me a hug and kiss on the cheek then sat down at the table after he noticed I was looking sad.

"Hey daddy."

"What's going on sweetie?" he asked.

I sighed, "I think Shy knows what happened to Rick and she is not saying anything."

"How do you figure she knows something?"

"Because it's this guy named Avery, who apparently doesn't like Rick, that Shy is cool with. I also saw Rick's roommate Lamar talking to him a couple of hours before we went to the police station. It's a lot of stuff going on and I am going to get to the bottom of it since nobody acts like they can tell me nothing."

"Hmmm. Did this Avery boy or Shy go in for questioning too?"

"No sir, just me and Rick's roommates."

"I definitely think they should both be questioned."

"Me too, I have Officer Anderson's card so I will be letting him know about what I have been noticing."

"Good idea sweetheart."

"How has Deon been Riah?" mom asked from the stove.

I looked at her and answered, "He's good for the most part."

"Good, guess the new prescription they prescribed him is working."

"Prescription?" I asked with a puzzled look on my face.

"Yes, around this time last year his mom said that he was acting a little strange, so she sent him to see a psychiatrist and they diagnosed him with bipolar disorder. The first pills they prescribed him didn't work as good because he wasn't acting like himself and always blowing up and what not. But I am glad to see that these new pills have him a little more on the calm side." I stared confusedly at her as she moved around the kitchen waiting for her to say more.

"Mariah?" dad said. I turned my attention to him, "Sir?"

"Looking a little big there sweetie." He said pointing at my stomach.

"Robert!" mom said in a stern voice.

"I'm just saying Denise, baby girl has been eating good up there at Livingston."

I sighed deeply, "Mom, dad, I have something to tell y'all." They both looked at me waiting on me to tell them what was going on.

"What's going on Mariah?" mom asked in a concern voiced.

"Yeah sweetie what's going on?" dad also asked in a concerned voice. They both continued to look at me until I finally lifted up my shirt and said, "Mom, dad, I'm ten weeks pregnant with Rick's baby." Mom had a shocked look on her face while dad sat there with a blank expression. He scratched his head then said, "Mariah if I hurt your feelings pointing out that you gained a little bit of weight since we've last seen you, I'm sorry, but, you don't have to joke with us like this."

"I'm not joking dad, I really am pregnant."

"What are you going to do with a baby? You're a 20 year old sophomore in college, you have your whole life and career ahead of you. A baby isn't what you need right now Mariah."

"I know dad but it takes two to make a child, and I knew the consequences so I have to deal with it."

"You don't have to deal with it Mariah."

"What do you mean by that?" I paused, "What, are you trying to tell me to get rid of my baby?"

"I'm just saying, know that you have options."

"Getting rid of my baby is not an option, especially since this is the only piece of Rick I will have," I said with an attitude.

"I just hope you know that if Rick was still here, my reaction would be the same."

"So what you're telling me that if I decide to keep the baby, which I plan on doing, you won't support me?

"I just want what's best for you Mariah."

I cut my eyes at him then turned my attention to mom who was back facing the stove, "Mom you haven't said anything this whole time, do you agree with dad?"

"Baby girl I'm just shocked," she replied. That did it for me, I stood up from the table, "I can't believe y'all aren't supportive of me. I've made my decision and I'm keeping the baby whether y'all support me or not." I grabbed my keys off of the table and walked to the front door. Before I walked out of the door mom stopped me, "I love you Mariah, this news is just a lot to take in. Once you become a mother you will understand the hurt your dad and I are feeling right now. We just want the best for you sweetie."

"Okay," I said then walked out of the door, got in my car and pulled off. When I got to the stop sign at the end of the road I began to cry, and decided to call Mr. Fuller.

"Hello," he answered.

"Hey pops." I sniffled, "I'm on my way over now."

"Oh alright. Are Shy and Deon with you too?"

"No just me."

"Mariah are you crying?"

No, I'm fine."

"You sure sweetie?"

"Yes, I promise."

"Alright well I'll be here waiting."

"Okay I'll see you in about five minutes."

"Alrighty."

"Bye."

I hung up the phone, made a left at the stop sign and proceeded to Mr. Fuller's house which was directly around the corner and down the street from my parents' house. I rung the door bell, and he answered the door wearing a gray sweater and blue jeans.

"What's the matter Mariah?" he asked looking right into my puffy eyes. I tried to hold it together but I couldn't anymore, "My parents." I said with tears rolling down my face. He put his arm around me and brought me in the house.

"What about your parents? Are they okay?" he asked once we were inside.

I slowed down my cries, "Yes they are fine, but we got into a disagreement before I came over here and it really hurt me." He started walking to the kitchen and motioned for me to follow him. He was finishing cooking, so I sat at the table while he finished.

"Well what was the disagreement about?"

I hesitated before I answered, "Umm, well I told them that I am 10 weeks pregnant with Rick's baby."

He stopped what he was doing, "Really?"

"I know you think I'm too young and I can't take care of a baby."

"No, this is the best news I could have received all weekend," he said with tears in his eyes He walked over to where I was sitting, "Just know that you won't be alone, I will help support you as if

Rick was still here. I feel like I've been given a second chance."

I looked at him, "What do you mean?"

"A second chance at being a better father, well in this case grandfather."

"Thank you pops, I really appreciate your support." I stood up and gave him a hug.

"No problem sweetie."

"Do you mind if I stay here tonight pops?" I asked after we stopped hugging.

"Of course I don't mind."

"Thank you."

Mr. Fuller and I spent the rest of that evening planning the rest of the funeral, talking about school, the baby, laughing, and eating. That man there knew he could throw down in the kitchen. I can still taste those ribs, greens, macaroni, yams, potato salad, cornbread, and blueberry muffins he made that night. The time slipped by and Mr. Fuller had went to bed after we cleaned the kitchen up. I went to the front room to watch TV and noticed that mine and Rick's favorite movie, Love and Basketball, was on. I fell asleep in the middle of the movie and had another dream about Rick. In the dream I was still at Mr. Fuller's house sitting on the couch watching the same movie.

"Rick hurry up its about to start."

Rick walked in the living room wearing all white and holding a bowl of popcorn, "I'm coming girl, we watch this movie everyday it seems like. You ain't tired of it yet?" he said as he got to the couch.

I reached for the bowl of popcorn and put some in my mouth, "Nope."

He sat on the couch right by me and placed his hand on my belly, "I missed you Riah."

"You only went to the kitchen to get popcorn and you missed me?"

He chuckled, "That's not what I mean." Then there was a moment of the dream where we were just staring at each other. Then he turned back and looked at the TV, "When are you going to tell Shy the good news?"

"I'm not." I responded with popcorn in my mouth.

"Why not?"

"I feel like I can't trust her right now."

"Shy is a good person Riah, there's no reason for you not to trust her. You know how crazy she is about us, she'll do anything to protect us." I shrugged at what he said then he pulled me by the chin and turned my face towards him and said, "Anything. Don't let something small get between y'alls friendship."

I woke up out of my sleep confused, trying to make sense of what all Rick was saying in the dream, but I couldn't really put together everything he said. I grabbed my phone from beside me to check the time and saw that it was two o'clock in the morning. The TV was still on, so I got the remote, turned it off and walked back to Rick's old room and went back to sleep.

REPASS

The day of Rick's funeral came, and it had been exactly a week since he died. It still hadn't fully registered to me that he was gone until I saw him laying lifeless in that casket. I couldn't hold it together at the funeral or at the burial site; I was a complete wreck. I didn't know if it was the hormones from the pregnancy or my regular emotions that had me so sad. Most of my emotions were based on the fact I would never see Rick again and my child would never physically know his or her father. I saw Shy and my parents at the funeral and cemetery but I didn't say anything to them, I haven't talked to any of them since Sunday. I haven't spoken to Deon since Sunday either. I text him Sunday night and let him know that I was going to stay with Mr. Fuller for the week to help get the house together, but he never responded. He didn't even show up for the funeral which was kind of weird. I hoped he would have at least came to the repass.

On the way back to Mr. Fuller's house from the burial site, I sat in the limousine and thought to myself how many people were at Rick's funeral. It filled my heart with joy to know that there were so many people he had an influence on. Everybody looked really nice wearing their green and white. Even though I was going through a lot more than many people knew, I decided that that day was not just about me, but everyone else who loved Rick. Because of that I was going to let my animosity against my parents and Shy go when I saw them at the repass;

We pulled up to Mr. Fuller's house first, and made our way inside. As others began to arrive, I stood off to the side in the middle of the living room and watched everybody come in. A lot of Rick's older relatives hugged and kissed me as they passed by. I was especially glad to see that Mr. Fuller's younger sister, Mrs. Keisha, and her husband Mr. Dezmond, made it in town to give pops some extra support. I got to know Rick's Aunt and Uncle well over the years. Their daughter Star was Rick's favorite first cousin. She was a little younger than us, and Rick loved to hang with her over the summers and the holidays, showing her the ropes as we grew up. He even taught Star how to play basketball. She became pretty good and eventually started to play for her school back.in Atlanta. I could tell she was taking his passing especially hard, as we embraced and comforted each other for a long time. We reminisced for a little while, and caught up on what was happening in each other's lives since we last spoke. By this time, several more people began to make their way into the house, so we hugged again, and agreed to catch up a little later.

The Bradley's and Monroe's came up and spoke to me before they went in the kitchen. Then I noticed my parents making their way over to where I stood.

"Mariah sweetie can we talk?" Mom asked once they made it to me.

"Yes." I replied softly.

"Look sweetie, me and your dad have been talking and maybe we over reacted to the news you told us Sunday. It was just a lot to take in at the time, but we decided that we are going to support you and the baby every step of the way."

"Yes...what your mother said. It's just that we just wanted better for you baby girl. We had you at a young age and it took us both a while to complete our degrees after you were born. We had to realize that our baby came first and everything else came second, including college. We both agreed that your mom would finish her degree first while I continued to work day and night to support our household. I guess what I'm trying to say is that your mother and I knew you wouldn't have that option since Rick isn't here to take that load off of your shoulders. But we know that you are a strong young lady and we are going to do whatever we can to support you and the baby," Dad chimed in.

I began to tear up, "Thank y'all for understanding." We all hugged.

"We love you sweetie," Dad said.

"I love y'all too," I said as Dad kissed me on the cheek then we stopped hugging.

"We are going to help Mr. Fuller in the kitchen; call for us if you need us," Mom said.

"Okay I will."

I watched them as they walked off towards the kitchen where Mr. Fuller, the Bradley's, Monroe's, and a couple other people were. As I turned my head back forward, I noticed Shy walking towards me. She was wearing a white dress with green heels.

"Hey Mariah," she said in a soft voice.

"Hey Shy," I said as I opened my arms for a hug.

She leaned into the hug, "I missed you Riah."

"I missed you too." We stopped hugging.

"I apologize for the whole Avery situation, I just want you to know there was nothing shady going on. He was just a guy I messed with on a regular. I cut him off the same day that you got mad at me because I refuse to let a nigga come between our friendship. I can go into details about it later if you want me to."

"Yeah we can talk about that later. I should have known you would not do anything to hurt me or Rick, so I accept your apology. Just don't keep anymore secrets from me."

"Okay that's cool, and I won't. I promise!" We stood there and talked for a minute then PJ and Jordan walked up to us, both wearing white suits with green ties.

"Sissss," PJ said, then he hugged me, "you good?"

"Yes, I'm good, thank you."

"Dang PJ you are going to suffocate my girl." Shy laughed then pinched PJ on the back, "Let her go." He stopped hugging me and turned around to Shy, "Shy don't be like that, you wish this was you I was hugging ain't it girl?" He started making kissy faces at her.

"Ewww, no!" she said holding her hand up to him.

"Okay, that is gross," Jordan said then hugged me. "Hey sis." He let me go then looked at Shy, "What's up Shy?"

"Hey, Jordan."

"Thank you Jordan for taking Deon's place and singing at the funeral," I said.

"No problem. Anything for my boy Rick."

Shy moved close to Jordan, "Yeah we didn't know you could sing like that."

PJ moved between Shy and Jordan and faced Shy, "If a singer is what you want baby then look no farther, I'm right here." He put his arm around Shy's shoulders, "I can sing too." He cleared his throat.

Shy moved from under his arm, "Move Percival, dang!" Me and Jordan stood there laughing at them.

PJ sucked his teeth, "Bruh y'all know I don't like nobody calling me by my government man." He looked at Jordan "Dawg, you think that's funny, huh?" he sucked his teeth again, "Forget y'all man, I'm bout to go in this kitchen and get on these beans, greens, potatoes, tomatoes, lamb, ram, hog, dog, beans, greens, potatoes, tomatoes, chicken, turkey, chicken..."

"You nameeee it!" Jordan shouted like he was in church. PJ and Jordan both laughed and walked off towards the kitchen.

"Mariah you want to go eat something?" Shy asked.

"Not right now, maybe a little later."

"Well you know black folks are greedy and they be quick to fix to-go plates, so I'm gone fix you a plate and ask Mr. Fuller to put it to the side for you."

"Okay, thank you."

Shy walked off to the kitchen to fix our plates. I stood there smiling as I scanned the house full of people laughing and conversing. It was beautiful to see everyone there celebrating the life of Rick. I looked back towards the front door and noticed that Deon had barged in wearing gray sweats and a black pull over sweater, the same outfit he had on the last time I saw him. It looked like his hair wasn't brushed, and he looked like he hadn't slept in days. His mom was on the way out of the kitchen and she saw him at the door and walked up to him. I couldn't really hear the conversation between them from where I stood, but Rick's Aunt Rosie was close by them and she ran the whole conversation back to me later.

"Deon baby, where have you been? We've been calling your phone. You weren't at your room and we've been looking all over for you," she said to him.

Mr. Bradley walked up to them, "Yeah son I don't like the way you are looking right now. What's wrong with you?"

Deon avoided eye contact with his parents and scanned the room, "Where's Mariah? I need to talk to her." I guessed he finally noticed me standing off to the side in the living room and walked over to me. I was a little scared at first, because I didn't know what was about to happen.

"Deon, what's wrong? Where have you been?" I asked once he got to me.

"I'm sorry Mariah, I haven't been myself lately, but I'm fine now. You're not mad that I missed the funeral are you?"

"I'm not mad Deon, I'm more so disappointed. You knew how important this day was, and for you to have missed it and coming in here looking like this, something must be wrong. So, tell me, what's wrong?"

"Nothing is wrong, I just haven't been myself this past week."

I leaned in towards him and whispered, "Have you been taking your pills?"

He backed up from me and had a shocked look on his face, "What pills?"

I reached and grabbed his hand before he stepped back anymore, "It's okay, I know you were diagnosed with bipolar disorder, you don't have to keep it a secret from me anymore."

He snatched his hand from me, "You don't know nothing!"

Mrs. Bradley walked up behind Deon and put her arms around his waste, "Baby let us take you home."

He pulled away from his mom, "I'm fine mom." Everybody in the living room was now looking at Deon suspiciously. Mr. Fuller heard raised voices from the kitchen and he saw the way Deon looked, so he came over to where we were.

"Deon!" he said furiously.

Mr. Bradley stood in front of Mr. Fuller before he got closer to Deon, "I got this. I'm sorry that he came into your home like this during this time." He turned and looked at Deon and Mrs. Bradley, "Let's go!" Mr. and Mrs. Bradley walked toward the front door, and walked out with Deon in the middle of them. Mr. Fuller shook his head with rage then made his way back to the kitchen. On the way back to the kitchen he passed Shy, PJ and Jordan who were standing in the doorway that connected the living room to the kitchen. I figured they saw everything that had just taken place from where they stood.

"I told y'all that nigga was weird." PJ whispered to Shy and Jordan.

Shy punched PJ in his arm, "That's not funny PJ. He's my friend." She walked back over to where I was. The same time that Shy was walking up to me Lamar walked up too. He must have come through the door right after Deon and his parents left because he wasn't there before.

"Mariah, can I talk to you please?" He asked.

"No!" Shy interjected.

He looked at Shy, "Nobody was talking to you Shy. Learn to be quiet sometimes, damn!" Shy stood there with her mouth open in disbelief that he just talked to her like that. He looked back at me, "I'm sorry, but can we please talk though? Alone?" I looked at Shy and gave her a nod to let her know to walk off, so I could hear what he had to say.

We watched her walk back to the kitchen then he looked at me, "I want to talk to you about what was going on with me the other day when you saw me talking to them guys."

"Okay I'm listening."

He sighed, "See man…"

PJ walked up just as Lamar was getting ready to talk, "Riah you good?" he asked, then mugged Lamar.

"Yeah PJ, I'm good, thank you."

"Nigga can't you see me and Riah were talking?" Lamar said.

"Can't you see I don't give a damn? I don't want no snakes close to my sis."

"Bro, this ain't the time or the place for this. We can handle what we got going on back at the room. Now go back to the kitchen and let me finish talking to Riah."

Jordan walked up, "Yo is everything good over here?" By the time Jordan finished his statement Shy had walked back up.

Lamar looked at PJ, Jordan, and Shy then sucked his teeth. Then he looked at me, "Riah I'll just catch up with you later man." He walked back to the front door and left.

"Snake ass nigga," Said PJ as he watched Lamar leave.

"Right! Anyways, Riah my mom wanted to ask you about school and stuff. You know she is a proud alumni," said shy.

"Okay where is she?"

"Yeah where is my mother-in-law?" PJ added.

Shy sucked her teeth then looked at Jordan, "Jordan get your boy before I knock him out in here."

Jordan laughed, "I got you." Shy grabbed me by the arm and we walked in the kitchen where her mom and my parents were sitting at the table.

"Mariah, how are you?" Mrs. Monroe asked once we got up to her. She stood up out of her chair and gave me a hug.

"I'm good." We stopped hugging and she offered me her seat.

"That's good to hear. So how is Livingston treating you?"

"Ehhh, could be better." I chuckled.

"Trust me, I know the feeling. Those professors do not play around up there."

"They sure don't."

"What is your major again?"

"Nursing."

"Nice. Following in your mom's footsteps."

"Yes ma'am."

"Well if you ever need anything while you are up there, let me know. I still have my connections in every department, and I know a few of the doctors at the hospitals up there personally."

"Thank you, Mrs. Monroe."

"Anytime sweetie. I'm trying to convince your friend over there to transfer up there." She looked at Shy after she said that.

"Ain't nobody trying to go way up there Ma," Shy said.

My mom laughed, "Why don't you want to go to Livingston, Shy?"

Shy looked at my mom, "Because, Mrs. Jones, I'm going to be too far away to get home cooked meals." She laughed, "My parents are a skip and a hop from Perry and all I have to do is pop up on them and grab a hot plate and whatever else I need." She laughed again.

My mom laughed, "You are a mess girl."

My dad laughed, "Yes she is."

"Ain't she? She knows how to cook but always seems to find her way to the house when we cook," Mrs. Monroe said.

Shy looked back at her mom, "I'm too cute to cook Ma." We all started laughing then Mr. Monroe, who was in the bathroom at the time, walked back in the kitchen and over to the table where we were.

"Girl you just lazy," he said.

Shy looked at her dad, "It be too much work Daddy...shoot."

Mr. Monroe laughed, "That's that lazy talk."

Shy laughed, "Daddy!"

"I'm just saying sweetie, your mama be the same way sometimes."

"Alright David. Whose side are you on?" Mrs. Monroe chimed in.

Mr. Monroe looked at Mrs. Monroe then at Shy then back to Mrs. Monroe, "I'm on the Lords side." We all laughed at his comment.

"Good choice my brother," my dad said to him.

The repass went on and a few more people who didn't make it to the funeral came by to pay their respects to the family. A good bit of people started packing to-go plates and leaving little by little as it started getting late. Shy's parents said their goodbyes, and hugged all of us as they left. Not too long after they left, my parents said their goodbyes as well, and hugged us all as they left too. PJ and Jordan stuck around for about 45 more minutes after my parents left and then they headed back to campus. After they left it was just Shy, Mr. Fuller, and I left at the house. We helped Mr. Fuller clean up the kitchen and the other areas of the house where people were. After we got finished cleaning, we all went to the living room to watch TV.

"I sure appreciate y'all for staying and helping me clean this place up."

"No problem, Mr. Fuller," Shy responded.

"Yeah pops, you know we got you."

He smiled and nodded at both of us then looked at me, "Mariah are you feeling alright baby girl?"

"Yes sir, I'm fine."

"Need anything else to eat or something?"

"Well, what I want I don't think you have it here."

"What's that?

I chuckled, "A Kool-Aid pickle."

He laughed, "Yeah, sorry baby girl don't have none of them 'round here." He and I both started laughing together.

"Girl why the heck you want a Kool-Aid pickle like you're pregnant or something?" asked Shy with confusion. Mr. Fuller and I stopped laughing and looked at each other, then I looked at Shy, "Shy I meant to tell you."

"Tell me what?

"I am ten, well, eleven weeks pregnant now."

She jumped off the couch and screamed with excitement, "For real?"

I laughed, "Yup."

She bent down and hugged me, "Oh my gosh Riah, I am so excited for you girl."

"You took that news just how I thought you would," I laughed.

She stopped hugging me and sat back beside me on the couch, "Girl you know I'm extra."

"This is true."

"I kind of figured you was pregnant though."

"How?"

"Girl you was looking thicker than usual and I know you don't eat heavy like that, so...yeah."

"Look at you being observant," I laughed. "So Shy, will you be the baby's God..."

She cut me off before I finished, "Girl of course I'll be the baby's God Mother! What kind of question is that?" she laughed then started rubbing my stomach.

Mr. Fuller laughed, "Girl, you are too silly."

I laughed with Mr. Fuller, "Ain't she though?"

Shy smiled, "What can I say?" Shy joined in with mine and Mr. Fullers laughs. Our laughs died down and Mr. Fuller asked, "Anybody know what was going on with Deon earlier? He didn't look like himself."

"He did look awful. That was my first time seeing him since he cooked me and Riah breakfast at his room Sunday morning. I've been hitting him up but he hasn't been responding to none of my texts or calls. I even went by his room but every time I went the door was locked or he wasn't there," Shy added.

"That's strange," he shook his head, "What about you Mariah, do you know what's going on with him?"

"Well Sunday after I left the police station, I went by my parents' house and my mom told me that he has been diagnosed with bi-polar disorder since around this time last year."

"What? Girl no!" Shy said with a shocked look on her face.

"Yes. My mom said that his mom was the one that sent him to go see a psychiatrist."

"Wow, not D!"

"Well that explains the reason he flipped the way that he did," said Mr. Fuller.

"My mom also said that he is on some kind of pills that are supposed to keep him calm. When he came up to me in the living room, I asked him did he take the pills and that's when he blew up."

"That's crazy man." Shy said.

"Yeah, it really is."

"I tell you one thing. If Deon's daddy stand in front of me like that again, I'm gone take him and his son on a first class flight with Fuller airlines," Mr. Fuller said. Shy and I both bursted out laughing at his comment.

"Mr. Fuller, you funny man," Shy said still laughing.

He laughed, "I'm trying to be like you young folks with the jokes."

"Oooo and you got the bars," she laughed, then looked at me. "Hey do you want to stay at my room for the weekend?"

"That's cool. I just need to go by my parents' house to grab some clothes." I looked at Mr. Fuller, "Is that cool with you, pops?"

"Go head baby girl. Think I'm about to call it a night anyways."

We all stood up off of the couch, I walked back to Rick's room and grabbed my bag that had my clothes I wore through the week in it, and we all walked to the front door. Mr. Fuller gave Shy and I hugs goodbye, then stood at the door watching as we got in our cars to leave. Shy came with me to my parents' house so she could help me carry some of the stuff I had inside. I was surprised that my parents were still up when we got there. I let them know that I was going to stay with Shy for the weekend and that I would be back home Sunday. I got everything I needed from the house, then

Shy and I headed to her room.

CLARITY, JEALOUSY, AND BETRAYAL

When we got back to Shy's room she told me that there was going to be a big party on campus that night and everybody was going to be there. I was kind of hesitant about going at first, but some way somehow, Shy ended up convincing me to go. I suggested to her that we go check on Deon before we went to the party and she agreed. We changed out of the clothes we wore to the funeral into some sweats and tennis shoes then walked to his room.

"Girl it's cold as fuck out here," Shy said rubbing her hands together, "I'm still wearing a dress to the party though."

"Girl you're gonna catch all the pneumoniasss tonight," I laughed.

She laughed, "Damn right. I'm gone catch a nigga while I'm at it too." I started laughing with her. Our laughs died down as we approached Deon's room. Luckily Deon's room wasn't too far from Shy's, because it was freezing outside. When we got to his door Shy jiggled the door knob to see if it was unlocked, but it wasn't so she knocked a couple of times. Without asking who it was, Deon answered the door still wearing the same clothes he had on earlier. He looked way better than he did when he was at the repass.

"Well dang Deon, you just gone answer the door and not ask who is it?" Shy asked.

"Naw, I figured it was y'all coming by to check on me," he said then moved to the side to let us in. We walked to the couch and sat down and he went and sat at the table after he closed the door.

"Well how are you feeling D?" I asked.

"I'm better now," he held his head down, "I'm sorry about how things went earlier."

"I assume you took your medicine once you got back here?"

He nodded, "Yes. Mom and Dad wouldn't leave until I did."

"D, why didn't you tell us about your diagnosis or that you are on medication?" Shy asked.

"Because, who wants a crazy friend?"

"You're not crazy Deon. You just have a condition that you have to learn to control," I said.

"Right, we love you D. We just want you to stay on top of taking your medicine, so you won't do anything you'll end up regretting," Shy added.

"I got you," he paused, "But aye Shy...you might want to tell boyfriend number 9 to watch himself, his name is coming up heavy at the station. Officer Anderson is trying to get him to come in for questioning but can't get in contact with him."

"Damn for real? Well he's not boyfriend number nine anymore so I guess that's none of my business."

I looked at Shy, "Is Avery boyfriend number nine?"

"Was boyfriend number nine. Past tense."

"Everybody wants to gang bang or be a drug dealer around here," Deon said.

"Shy, were you helping him sell drugs?" I asked.

She screwed up her face, "What? Girl hell no. We just smoked together here and there."

I let out a sigh of relief, "Oh girl I was about to say. You had me nervous for a minute there."

"Girl you should know better than that." She checked the time on her phone, "Girl we need to head back to my room so we can get dressed."

Anthony Taylor

"Dressed? Where y'all going?" Deon asked.

"Some party on campus that Shy convinced me to go to with her," I replied.

"At the Cove?"

"Yessir!" Shy answered.

He chuckled, "Have fun with that. I'm probably going to grab some food in a while then come back here and get myself together some more."

"Good idea," I said. Shy and I got up off of the couch, hugged Deon, and started walking to the door. Shy walked out the door before me, and before I made it out the door all the way Deon grabbed my hand, and I turned around and looked at him.

"Ummm, do you think after the party you could come back here and stay with me?" he asked.

"I would, but I already told Shy I would stay with her, but I can come by in the morning."

He made a fake smile, "Okay, have fun. See you in the morning." He let go of my hand.

"See you." I walked out of his room and caught up with Shy, he closed and locked the door behind me. We ran back to Shy's room to get out of that cold. When we got back, we snatched off our sweat suits and pulled out our outfits that we were going to wear to the party. Shy put on a short red skin tight dress with some strappy heels and silver jewelry. I put on a long gold and tan dress with gold heels. After we got dressed we both stood in the bathroom mirror and looked at each other. Shy pulled out her make-up bag and started doing her make-up in the mirror.

"Oooooo Riah...girl, you got a fine best friend you hear me."

I stood there looking sad at myself in the mirror, "I don't like my outfit." I put both my hands on my stomach, "I look fat."

She looked at me in the mirror, "Riah please don't start, you are not fat. Girl you're only eleven weeks pregnant and still look good; you're just thick in all the right places."

"I don't need to be going to a party anyways Shy, I'm pregnant."

"Riah it's an on campus party so it won't get too wild. You act like we going to Lava or something. You'll be fine, I promise. Whenever you are ready to leave and come back to the room, we can leave."

"You right...okay."

"I know I'm right. Now come in my room so I can find something out of my closet for you to wear." She put the last finishing touches on her make up then we walked in her room. I sat on her bed while she looked through her closet. I pulled off my heels then reached in my purse and pulled out Rick's phone.

"Girl I can't believe it's been a whole week since Rick was killed and they still haven't found out who killed him," I said.

"Right. Trash ass police."

"Right. I'm still stuck on the fact that the person who killed Rick took his damn laptop."

"Right! Like what the fuck are you going to do with a laptop? I'm sure it has a password on it so whoever has it won't be able to use it anyways."

"Yeah it did. There were a few other personal things that nobody but Rick needed to see on there. That's one of the biggest reasons I want to get that back."

Shy turned her head around and looked at me, "Personal things like what?"

I smiled at her, "You know...personal things."

She scrunched her face up and laughed, "You nasty."

"Look who's talking." We both laughed then she turned her head back around to keep looking for something for me to wear, and I started looking back through Rick's phone.

"Whatever! But hey...you should consider using find my Mac, if that's a real thing."

I looked up from the phone, "I think it is. If so, I'm going to do that tonight after the party."

"Okay cool. So have you heard back from Officer Anderson or anybody at the station?"

"No not since Sunday."

"Oh okay. I saw Lacy the other day when I was walking to class and she stopped me and told me that Officer Anderson made her come in on Tuesday for questioning."

"For real? Did she say what they asked her?"

"Basically the same questions they asked y'all." She turned her head and looked at me, "But see I'm gone tell you why it couldn't have been her that killed Rick."

"Oh yeah?"

"Mmhhhmm."

"This ought to be good."

She turned completely around from the closet facing me then clapped once, "Okay so boom! I'm about to hit you with some Shyology. So last Saturday she was at work at our favorite spot when we went up there right?"

"Right."

"Then didn't PJ tell us that she was supposed to come over to their room to wait for him there when they got back from Lava the night Rick died?"

"Yeah..."

She clapped once again, "But she didn't go to their room that night because she did have to be to work in the morning."

"But how do you know that she didn't go to the room still even though she said that she wasn't going to go?"

"Because her and Chelsea are roommates, and I was over there in their room doing Chelsea's hair from like eleven to right before you called me and told me what happened, and I heard her in her room snoring the paint off of the walls. She got home from work like twelve, showered and took her ass to sleep," Shy said as she turned back around to the closet.

"Look at you cracking cases girl," I laughed.

She laughed, "Right. I should've been a Criminal Justice major instead of nursing, hell."

"Sure."

She pulled an all black jumper out of the closet then turned around to show me, "What you think about this?"

"Oh that's cute, I'll wear that."

"Bet." She took the outfit off the hanger and handed it to me. I laid it on the bed, took off what I had on, and put on the black jumper. She gave me some gold accessories to put on and I put my heels back on. I did a 360 in front of Shy, "How do I look?"

"Girl, fine as fuck."

"I might have to keep this then girl," We both laughed.

"Come on girl, let's head to the Cove.

"Okie dokie." We walked out of the room and headed to the party.

I didn't believe Shy when she said that the whole campus would be at the party until we got there and we saw damn near all the students in attendance. There was a line to get in but it moved pretty fast, so we were not outside long. As soon as we got inside the party, we found a clear spot and started dancing. The DJ played a lot of good songs that had everybody in the crowd vibing. While I was dancing, I looked to my left and saw Jordan through the crowd dancing with a girl, then I looked a little to the right of him and saw PJ also dancing with a girl. PJ saw Shy and moved the girl he was dancing with out of the way and tried to come dance with Shy, but she saw him coming towards us so she grabbed me and we walked away. Once we got to another clear spot, a song I really liked came on and I started dancing.

"Yes bitch, I see you!" Shy yelled and hyped me up while she watched me dance. She pulled out her phone and started recording me.

"Don't have me out here getting it by myself Shy." I stopped dancing and grabbed her phone and recorded her while she danced. After that song went off Shy came and stood by me and we started laughing. Then she saw someone in the crowd and started tapping me on the shoulder really fast.

"Oh shit girl."

"What?"

She stopped tapping me, "Marco's fine ass is here!"

"Who is Marco?"

"Girl Marco Reynolds!" She pointed at a tall guy who was standing off to the side by himself wearing a white sweater, blue jeans and a white hat.

"Who is he?" I asked.

"He's on the basketball team and his mom is a professor here too. I been trying to holla at his fine ass for a little minute now."

I laughed, "Girl you a mess, I swear."

"I'm serious Riah!" she laughed, "I dropped one, so now I gotta add one."

"Here you go. So what are you going to do?"

"I want to go talk to him since he is standing by himself right now, but I don't want to leave you standing here by yourself."

"Girl go head, I'll be straight right here."

"You sure?"

"Yes girl, I'm good I promise, go head."

"Okay! I'll be back in five minutes. I'm just gone ask him for his number then come right back."

"Okay." She gave me a hug and walked through the crowd to get to Marco. I pulled out my phone and just stood there while people danced around me. Then I felt somebody back into me so I turned around to see who it was. I turned around and I was looking at the person's back until he turned around and faced me, and I saw that it was Lamar. He had a water bottle full of alcohol in his hand and there were two girls standing behind him both wearing short black dresses and black heels. One of the girls had long braids and the other had long straight hair.

He slurred, "Riah! What's good sis." He leaned down and gave me a hug.

"Hey Lamar."

"Damn Lamar, this what the fuck you doing!" the girl with the braids exclaimed.

"Yeah nigga you real disrespectful," the straight hair girl added.

He leaned up from hugging me then turned back towards them, "Man shut y'all ass up 'cause it ain't even like that. This Rick's girl."

"Ohhhh, hey how are you?" The straight hair girl asked as she walked around Lamar to come hug me. I stood there with my arms by my side and a blank expression on my face.

"I'm good." I answered her dryly then she stopped hugging me and backed up.

"It's nice to meet you," said the girl with the braids.

"Same," I responded to her dryly too.

Lamar looked at both the girls, "Aye y'all, look, let me talk to Mariah for a minute. I'll catch up with y'all in a few." They both said "Okay," then Lamar took a big sip of whatever was in the water bottle, and gave it to the girl with the straight hair. The two girls waved bye to me and walked off through the crowd and Lamar stood there watching them.

I tapped him on his arm to get his attention, "So what's up? What do you need to talk to me about?"

He leaned down, "I want to explain something to you but it's kind of loud in here. Do you mind stepping outside to talk? I know its cold outside, so I won't be long."

"Sure, I guess." He leaned back up, put his right arm around my shoulder and walked through the crowd splitting people with his left arm. We made it out of the party and walked over to a bench not too far from the party and sat down.

He sighed, "Alright, so I need to clear my name, I know shit been looking real sketchy lately but I promise it's not like that."

I folded my arms, "Why should I believe you Lamar? You have been acting real different this last week and it had me thinking that you had something to do with Rick's murder.

"I can assure you that I didn't kill Rick and you don't have to believe me now, but at least just hear me out." He paused and looked at me, "Please?"

"Okay, I'm listening."

He took a deep breath, wiped his face, and sighed, "Iight so... coming up back home in Shiloh, I use to be in the streets real heavy and the only thing that really kept me out of the streets was basketball. I didn't even expect to go to college, but when I was offered a basketball scholarship to come play here, I took it because I figured it would possibly be a new start for me. When I got here and met Rick, we clicked off rip because he knew about that street life and we related on that level. I felt like he was the only one who understood me. Rick did tell me how he gave that life up before he came to Perry and he tried to convince me to let it go all the way. I was definitely considering it until I met Avery, and when I saw he was on that gang bang shit, it opened my mind back up to it, and I wanted part of it. I started kicking it with Avery more and more not knowing he was a part of the rival gang that Rick use to be part of. He eventually introduced me to Greg and Aaron, the two guys who were with him when you saw me the other day. Greg was the guy with the dreads, and Aaron was the short bald nigga. I kept stressing to Avery how I wanted to run with him and his gang and he was down, but of course, I had to do some shit to get initiated." He sighed and wiped his face again, "On the night Rick was killed before the actual murder happened, we was all in the room getting ready to go to Lava and I was texting Avery about what I needed to do to get in the gang, and he said that night was a good night since we were off. He hit me back telling me to pull up to his crib around 1:30-2 and bring my ski mask, so I did. Me, PJ, and Jordan tried to convince Rick to go out with us, but he wasn't fucking with it. He said he'd rather talk on the phone with you. PJ and Jordan rode to Lava together and I told them that I was going to drive separate because I had some other shit going on that night. I left Lava at a decent time to make sure I got to Avery's spot at the time that he said. When I walked in the house it was him, Greg, and Aaron standing around a table that had black tape, two guns, and some rope on it. They were dressed in all black. I looked at all the stuff on the table, then looked at them and asked 'what are we about to do?'

Greg was like 'Nigga we about to rob somebody!'

And Avery quickly chimed in to say 'Not just anybody...we about to rob your boy Rick.'

So of course I'm surprised as hell and I'm asking, 'Rick???'

And that fool Aaron is like 'Hell yeah nigga, Rick, your roommate!'

I looked at the stuff again then looked at them boys, and was like 'Naw y'all, I can't even do that shit.'

At this point, Avery is getting irritated and snapping at me, talking about 'Nigga if you want to be a part of this gang, you gotta do some gang shit. So what the fuck you gone do Lamar?'

I stood there quiet for a minute looking at the stuff on the table, then I looked up at Greg and Aaron, then I looked at Avery. Ughhhh...the peer pressure got to me, so I finally was like, 'I'm in man.'

Lamar paused for a moment as he began to tense up, then he finally bursted out in an agitated tone, "Fuck man! I can't even believe I was there, and I was thinking at that time...how did I get myself in this predicament??? My body was in turmoil and I really didn't know what to do. Ughh...I messed up, I messed up!"

At this moment I'm intently listening, and hoping he is going to tell me something to find out who killed Rick. I began to urge him to continue with his story, "so what happened next?"

Lamar calmed his nerves, and continued, "I stood there watching while they put the stuff from the table in a black book bag. Then we all went outside and got in Aaron's car. Aaron got in the driver's seat, and Avery got in the passenger seat. I sat behind Aaron and Greg sat behind Avery. Aaron crunk the car up, and we headed to campus. A lot of thoughts were going through my head while I sat in that back seat man. Like...did I really want to turn on my boy to be a part of some shit that he don't even fuck with??? Every second in that car felt like minutes of agony. I knew I couldn't do it man, not to my boy Rick. I told Aaron to stop the car and let me out. So now these dudes are pissed at me.

Aaron is scowling at me and yelled out 'What nigga?!'

At this point I'm yelling too, and I'm like 'Stop the fucking car nigga! I can't do this shit!'

Avery turned around in his seat and looked at me, 'Fuck you mean you can't do this shit?'

Now I'm only getting more mad and I'm like, 'Dawg I can't go through with robbing Rick. That's my boy and if I rob him that'll be some slaw shit on my end, so I'd rather not have that on my conscience.'

Avery is staring at me from the front seat, and still trying to put the pressure on me and threatening me, 'Nigga if you back out you might as well cancel your chances in this shit my nigga.'

Now my blood is starting to boil over more and more. I ain't with nobody tryna hold no shit over my head and I told that nigga 'Fuck this shit honestly bruh. It ain't even worth it.'

I wasn't about to keep going back and forth with these niggas, so I just looked out the window of the car at this point.

Avery turns back around in the seat, and tells Aaron, 'Pull over cuz.'

Aaron's punk ass gone ask Avery, 'You sure?'

This bitch Avery talking shit like 'Yeah, let this soft ass nigga out.'

Of course, Aaron's dumb ass is going to do as told, so he's like, 'Shit, iight bruh.'

Aaron pulled the car over and when I reached for the handle of the door my phone started ringing, so I let go of the handle and reached in my pocket to pull out my phone. When I got my phone out my pocket I saw it was Jordan calling so I answered.

'Yo J, what's good?'

J sounds upset and was like 'Lamar nigga where you at man? Where you at man? Rick man Rick.'

I'm like, 'Wait, wait, Jordan slow down bruh, I can't understand what you trying to say.

Maaan...the next words out his mouth crushed me. Jordan was like 'Bruh... Rick's dead bruh! Rick dead man! Rick's DEAD!!!'

Jordan just kept saying it again and again and he's crying hysterically.

I was so overwhelmed I didn't know what to do. It was like someone sucked the breath out of me. I just punched the back of the driver seat, and I'm asking Jordan, 'Bro...where y'all at?'

J's like, 'On campus at the room bruh.'

So immediately I tell him, 'Iight, I'm on my way!'

I hung up the phone and started crying in my hands. I'm back there bawling crying! I can see out the corner of my eye that Avery turned around looking at me with a stunned face.

Avery's asking, 'Nigga what happened?'

I took my hands down from my face, 'Man somebody just fucking killed Rick.'

This shit was crazy. Even Greg was like, 'Bruh, what the fuck?'

Aaron is baffled too, and said, 'That's crazy man.'

Greg bursts out, 'Hell yeah!'

Avery just sat in the front seat looking on his phone not saying anything. Man that mess pissed me off so bad; I could have choked his ass right then and there. I yelled at Aaron to take me back to my car, so I could head to campus and Avery nodded at him to do it. Riah, that call fucked me ALL the way up man." Lamar shook his head, then looked at me, "I know what all I told you still doesn't make me look any better but I just wanted you to know that I wasn't the one who killed Rick. That day you saw me talking to Avery and them they were trying to convince me to come on another mission with them, but I told them that I wasn't with all that shit anymore after you had walked off. I don't even talk to them boys anymore really."

I sighed with relief then looked at him, "Well it's good to know that you are not the one who killed Rick, and that you decided to not hang with them anymore, but it is pretty fucked up that you were still going to go through with robbing Rick though."

"Yeah bruh, that was fucked up that you still got in the car with them boys," Jordan said from behind me and Lamar.

"Yeah nigga, fuck were you thinking?" PJ chimed in. Lamar and I turned our attention to where PJ and Jordan were standing at.

"How long y'all been standing there?" Lamar asked.

"Long enough nigga!" PJ said aggressively.

Jordan put his hand on PJ's shoulder, "Chill P." He looked at Lamar, "But we were leaving the party, about to head back to the room and we saw y'all sitting over here so we walked up to see if everything was good. When we got to y'all, you was saying how you was texting Avery before we went to Lava."

Lamar sighed, "So y'all pretty much heard everything?" He shook his head and sighed again, "Look man..."

PJ cut Lamar off, "Ain't no look nigga! You was bout to rob a nigga who you claim was your boy for what? Some damn colors and recognition? You lame as fuck nigga and I mean that!"

Lamar stood up off of the bench, "Nigga I already feel bad enough for the decision I made so you ain't gotta come out here and rub that shit in my face no more."

"Fuck that shit nigga! You a fucking snake and ain't no justifying it."

"Y'all boys calm down," Jordan said.

"Naw J, I'm 'bout to beat this snake ass nigga dawg."

"Wassup then nigga?!" They started walking towards each other and I got up off of the couch and stood in the middle of them, "Calm down y'all." I looked at Lamar, "Sit down, Lamar." He sat down then I looked at PJ, "Calm down PJ, please."

"I got you sis," PJ responded.

I sat back down on the bench, "Thank you." I looked at Lamar again, "Look Lamar, I appreciate you opening up and telling me that and it's a good thing that Jordan and PJ were standing here too so they could know what's going on. It may take me a little minute to fully forgive you about the decision you made and y'all can handle it how y'all do, but that's neither here nor there. What I'm focused on now is that the killer of my boyfriend is still out here walking around freely."

"I got you. I want to do what I can to help you find out who killed him," Lamar said.

"You honestly did enough Lamar. You gave us a lead on who it possibly could be. Although you were with Avery, he could've still said something to one of his gang brothers or whatever they call them about him robbing Rick, and somebody could have got to him first."

He held his head down, "True." I was about to get ready to say something else but I felt dizzy. I grunted and grabbed my head.

Jordan ran up to me and put his hands on my shoulders, "Riah you good?"

"Yeah, I'm just a little light headed. Think I need to go lay down."

"Where you staying tonight?"

"With Shy but she locked her room door when we left to come over here. So I'll probably hit Deon up to sit there until Shy gets done partying, since he is at his room."

"You sure you just don't want to come to our room?"

"Yeah it's cool. I need to tell Deon the information Lamar just told me anyways and maybe that can help with finding out who killed Rick."

"I got you."

I pulled my phone out of my purse and called Deon. The phone went straight to voicemail so I left a message, "Hey D, I'm leaving the party early to come to your room. I'm not feeling too good, so I'm just gone come lay down until Shy leaves here. See you soon." I hung up the phone, and said, "I'm gone text him too just to make sure he knows I'm coming." After I sent a text to Deon, Lamar and Jordan helped me off of the bench.

"Since me and Jordan was leaving anyways, we'll walk you to Deon's room. It's on the way to our new room anyways," PJ said.

"Thanks y'all."

"Told you, we got you sis," Jordan said.

I smiled at PJ and Jordan, then looked at Lamar, "Can you tell Shy that PJ and Jordan are walking me to Deon's room, and if she can, come by there to get me whenever she leaves here."

"I got you."

"Thank you."

Lamar walked off to head back inside the party to let Shy know what I said, then PJ and Jordan walked with me towards Deon's room.

"So, Riah." PJ said.

"What's up?"

"What's up with your girl Shy man?"

"What you mean?"

"Why she be playing hard to get man?"

I laughed, "I don't know. You know she a hard body."

"And I can deal with that. All she got to do is give a nigga a chance."

"I hear you PJ."

He laughed, "I'm serious sis. Put in a word for your boy. Tell her it's cold out here and she need a big nigga like me to keep her warm."

I laughed, "You are silly, but I got you."

"'Preciate it sis."

We arrived to Deon's room door and I knocked a couple of times but I didn't get an answer.

"You sure he here Riah?" Jordan asked.

"Yeah he said he wasn't doing anything tonight besides going to get food so I figured he would be here. I'm going to try calling him again." I pulled out my phone and tried calling him a second time, but his phone went to voicemail again.

"Still no answer?" PJ asked.

"Naw. I wonder why his phone keeps going to voicemail though. It's weird."

"Well, I mean he is weird."

I chuckled, "Shut up PJ."

Jordan twisted the door handle to see if it was open and it was. "Well the door is open," he said opening the door all the way for me to walk in.

"You good sis?" PJ asked.

"Yes. Thank y'all again."

"No doubt. How long are you going to be here on campus?" asked Jordan

"I'll be here the whole weekend."

"Bet. Well we have a game tomorrow you should slide."

"Cool. What time does it start?"

"Girls start at four and we tip off at 6:30," PJ responded.

"Okay cool, I'll be there."

I gave them both hugs and told them I would see them tomorrow before they walked off. I closed the door and when I turned around, I saw Deon's room keys on the counter, so I didn't lock the door. I walked from the front room to Deon's bedroom to see if he might've been in there sleep, but he wasn't. I looked around his room with a face of disappointment because of how messy it was.

I was going to try to lay on the bed but there was too much stuff on it, so I just walked over to the desk. I pulled the chair out and saw a black skully on top of a laptop that had a file folder inside of it. I took that stuff out of the chair, put it on the desk then sat down and took off my heels. I looked up, scanned the room then looked back down at the stuff I just laid on the desk. There was a paper sticking out of the file folder that had the name "Richard Fuller" in the corner of it. I raised one eyebrow and stared confused at that paper wondering what it was. Meanwhile while Jordan and PJ were walking to their room, they saw Shy leaving the party and walked up to her.

"Sup Bae," PJ said to her.

She put her hand up at him, "Boy please!" She looked at Jordan, "Y'all already walked Riah to Deon's room?"

"Yeah we did."

"Okay thanks. I'm 'bout to head that way now. Y'alls boy Lamar lit as hell too. He in there with them two chicken heads."

"Yeah, I noticed that."

"Nigga acting like we ain't got a game tomorrow and shit," PJ said.

"Right! But aye Shy I'm not sure if Deon was at his room or not though. Mariah was calling his phone but she said it was going straight to voicemail. When we got to his room I twisted the door handle and it was unlocked."

"That's weird," Shy said.

"Guess nobody listens to PJ when I say the nigga is weird." PJ said.

"Shut up P," Jordan said pushing PJ.

"I'm just saying J, Riah just said he was weird and now Shy saying it." He clapped once, "The." He clapped again, "Nigga." He clapped once more, "Is." He clapped a fourth time, "Weird."

"You sickening boy!" Shy said.

"Hell, there go his weird ass right there," PJ said pointing at Deon who was walking back in the direction of his room with a bag in his hand. Shy and Jordan turned around and watched him as he walked briskly to the room.

"Nigga moving with a purpose ain't it?" Jordan said.

"Hell J, its cold as fuck out this bitch." PJ said.

Jordan laughed and rubbed his hands together, "Is." They both laughed then looked at Shy who stood quiet and was still looking at Deon walk until she couldn't see him anymore.

"Yo Shy, you good?" Jordan asked.

"Yeah." She paused, "Y'all walk with me to Deon's room."

"Iight."

All three of them started walking to Deon's room with Shy leading the way. Back in Deon's room, I was still sitting there looking at the paper with Rick's name on it. I slowly reached for the black skully on top of the laptop, and held it in front of me. When I held it up, I saw that it was a ski mask, the same one the person who killed Rick had on. I had a quick flashback to that night when the person in the ski mask closed Rick's laptop. I went to go place the ski mask on the desk and as I was doing it, I noticed that the laptop on the desk was Rick's. My eyes grew wide and I put my left hand over my mouth as I stared at the laptop in shock. I took my hand from my mouth and opened Rick's laptop. I pulled the file folder out, examined it and found the police report from Rick's murder inside of it.

"Oh my gosh." I paused, "Oh my fucking gosh," I said to myself softly. My heart started pounding through my chest, the same way it did the night Rick was murdered. I can't even believe what I am seeing right in front of my eyes! Fear and panic begin to kick in. I'm in shock, and my mouth is wide open, as I'm astounded by what I've found. I softly ask myself, "What the HELL is going on???" My heart dropped at the thought that Deon could have something to do with Rick's murder, and here I am in his room alone. I need to get out...

"Riah?" Deon said, with a distraught look on his face.

I jumped a little, but I quickly tried to gather myself. Once I turned around, I saw him standing there with a bag of food in his hand. It felt like every hair on my body stood up, and the sound of his deep voice made me cringe, as if I felt every decibel travel down my spine when he called my name.

I'm thinking, I have to try to mask my fear. I timidly say, "Oh hey, D."

"Wha, what are you doing here? I thought you were going to the party and staying with Shy tonight?"

"I did go to the party, but I left because I wasn't feeling good so I came here because Shy was still partying. I called your phone twice but it went straight to voicemail both times. When I got here your door was unlocked, so I just came in."

"Oh okay." He paused then walked in the room more and saw that Rick's laptop was open, "So what were you doing?"

I looked down at the file folder in my lap then looked at him, "Deon?"

"Yeah?"

By this time, Shy, Jordan, and PJ had walked into Deon's room and stood in the front area, quietly listening to the conversation between Deon and I.

"What is this? Why do you have Rick's laptop? How did you get this police report?"

"Riah... I..."

"Deon what the FUCK is going on?!" My eyes started tearing up.

He stood there and looked at me, "Riah... I didn't mean to, I swear. I'm sorry. I..."

I stood up out of the chair and threw the whole file folder at him, "You didn't mean to what Deon!? Are you saying you...?"

"I'm so sorry."

"No, no, no, noooo," I bursted into tears and sat back in the chair putting my head in my lap. Shy, PJ and Jordan were in the front room flabbergasted at what they just heard. Shy was crying softly and PJ and Jordan both were breathing heavy with their fists bald up.

Shy put her hand over her mouth, "Oh my fucking gosh. I can't believe what I just heard." Jordan walked up to Shy and hugged her. She put her head in his chest while she cried.

"Man what the fuck!" PJ said in a low angry voice.

"I can't believe this nigga killed Rick man," Jordan whispered.

"Man I'm about to go grab this nigga J," PJ started walking in the direction of Deon's room.

Shy leaned off of Jordan, "PJ wait."

"Wait for what Shy? This nigga killed Rick man."

"I know but you don't want to walk in and startle him 'cause he could possibly hurt Riah. Let me step out and call the police right quick."

"Iight."

PJ walked back closer to Jordan and Shy walked out of the front door quietly. PJ and Jordan stayed inside to listen to the rest of what went on in the room with Deon and I.

Deon put his food on his bed, walked up to me and tried to put his hand on my back, "Riah man I'm sorry...I..." I stood back up out of the chair and pushed him. He stumbled backwards and bumped into the edge of his bed.

I yelled, "Sorry is not going to bring my fucking boyfriend back!"

He gathered himself together, "Riah..."

"What, happened?"

"Riah that's not important."

I began to holler at him, "Tell me what happened! Why the fuck did you kill Rick?"

He sighed deeply, "I was so hurt back then. That Valentine's Day, freshman year. I went all out and bought you that big ass 50-dollar bear. I was gonna ask you to be my girlfriend. But then Rick and Shy showed up, and he asked you first. You dropped my gift on the floor to get his. You chose him over me. I was just so hurt. I was there first. I loved you first. I tried to let it go, but seeing y'all together just made it worse, made me so angry. I was so jealous, the more I saw y'all together the more jealous I got. But I put on a fake smile every time. You was my best friend and I thought maybe just having that would be enough.

Then you went off to Livingston and I thought things would get better between me and Rick, but they didn't. He started hanging more with his basketball teammates and kicked me to the curb, so I started doing my own thing. I got more involved with the campus police and started doing more work at the forensic science office.

Then last year I was diagnosed with bipolar disorder and my mom took me to a psychiatrist who prescribed me these pills. That first prescription had me all the way fucked up, like it messed up my head. I mean like, I wasn't myself at all. That memory of you dropping my gift for Rick's, choosing him over me, just kept playing over and over in my head. I wanted to hurt him man. I wanted to get back at him, but I didn't know how I was going to do it.

So I... I was following Rick to see how I could make a move on him, but he was always with somebody. That Monday before I-I... killed Rick, I was prescribed some new pills and they made me a little more calmer, but it was too late. It was like my mind was already made up, I couldn't stop myself. I knew that Friday night that the basketball team was off the whole weekend and I figured that they would all be trying to go out that night. So my plan was, I was going to sneak in their room and wait for him there, just to shake him up a little.

When I got to the room I didn't expect the door to be unlocked, but it was so I walked in. But I heard him on the phone with you and that threw my whole plan off. I walked by the room the first time to see which way he was facing and that's when you saw me and he called out 'Yo.' The second time I walked by and looked in the room and noticed he wasn't even paying attention. I was going to walk out, but I figured I would just tussle with him a little to shake him up. That's when I started making the noise with the pots and pans, to get him to come out there. When he came to the kitchen he came straight at me on some hostile shit and some way he had took my ski mask off. He looked so disappointed when he saw my face. I didn't know what to do. How was I gonna explain myself. I ain't know what else to do. I just, I killed him.

It was hard watching him stumble back to the room but I figured you were still on facetime so I put the mask back on and I came in the room, stepping over all that blood, and got the laptop and left. That Saturday you came down, when I told you I was running errands, I was at the station getting the police report while Officer Anderson was here on campus."

"So you killed the father of my child because you were jealous and wanted revenge?" I asked angrily.

"I...," he paused and looked at me confused, "Father of your child?"

"Yes." I cried, "I'm pregnant."

"Since when?"

"Since eleven weeks ago."

He walked towards me, "Riah..." I backed up away from him still crying. I sat on the desk because I couldn't back up anymore.

He reach out to me for a hug, "Riah it's okay, you don't have to raise the baby alone. We can raise the baby together. Be my girl-friend."

I looked at him in disgust, "What?" then I pushed him, "Deon get your crazy ass away from me!"

He hit the side of the bed then looked at me with an angry look on his face, "Don't call me crazy." He started walking back towards me, "I'm not fucking crazy."

I held my arms out, "Deon get away from me."

He grabbed me by the arms, "I'm not fucking crazy."

"Let me go."

"I'm not fucking crazy."

PJ, Jordan, and Shy were still in the front room listening. Shy walked back in when Deon was telling me what happened leading up to him killing Rick. They heard me telling Deon to get off of me, over and over.

PJ whispered angrily, "Bruh, fuck this shit! I'm going in there." He ran in Deon's bedroom, grabbed Deon off of me and threw him on the bed and started punching him. I got off of the desk and ran to the hallway and met Shy and Jordan. They both put their arms around me and we walked to the front room. Once we got to the front room Shy and I started hugging each other and crying while Jordan rubbed both of our backs.

"Deon killed Rick, Shy." I said between cries.

"I know. We walked in when he was telling you what happened."

"Why though, Shy?"

"Jealousy man."

We both stood there and cried more. PJ and Deon were still in the room fighting but somehow, they ended up in the hallway. When they got in the hallway PJ slipped and fell and Deon got on top of him and started choking him. Jordan saw Deon choking PJ and ran over to them and grabbed Deon off of PJ and pinned him on the floor. Deon pushed Jordan off of him, got up and put Jordan in a choke hold on the wall. Shy and I saw him choking Jordan.

"Deon, stop!" I yelled. Then I grunted, grabbed my head and started falling to the floor.

Shy caught me before I hit the floor, "Riah!"

Deon noticed that I was hurt and let go of Jordan and tried to walk over to where I was, but PJ got up off the floor and grabbed him and held him in a bear hug from behind. Jordan ran over and helped Shy put me on the couch. I could still hear everything that was going on I just couldn't get out any words.

"Riah?" Jordan called out to me then checked my pulse, "Shit she still got a pulse, I think she just passed out. Call the ambulance or somebody."

Shy cried, "The police should be on their way soon. I'm going to call again so they can send an ambulance though." She dialed the police again and asked for an ambulance.

"Police?" Deon yelled from the hallway.

"Yeah nigga! Your ass going to jail tonight cuz," PJ said.

Deon started head butting PJ in the nose until he let him go. Once Deon was freed, he ran past us and out of the front door.

Shy was still crying, "Riah, please get up! Please!"

"Come on Riah." Jordan said.

My eyes fluttered open and I saw Jordan and Shy both leaning over me then they closed again. I still wasn't able to speak or really move like that, but I could still hear what was going on. Jordan, Shy, and PJ nurtured me until the police and paramedics arrived to Deon's room. Two policemen and two paramedics showed up approximately ten minutes after Shy made the second call. When they came in the room the paramedics came over to me, put me on the gurney and wheeled me to the ambulance. PJ, Jordan and Shy stayed behind in the room to talk to the police.

A tall officer with the curly hair walked up to Shy, "Hello ma'am my name is Officer Peters and this is Officer Davis. We're here responding to a murder suspect call. Can you tell us where the suspect is and answer a few questions?"

"Hello. Yes, his name was Deon Bradley. He ran off like a couple minutes before y'all got here."

He pulled out a pad and started writing notes, "Okay. So can you tell me what happened ma'am?" Shy was about to speak but was cut off by one of the paramedics coming back in the room. He looked around and asked, "Whoever is riding to the hospital with the young lady please follow me to the ambulance."

Shy looked at the officers and spoke quickly, "Those two guys over there," she pointed at PJ and Jordan, "They saw and heard everything they should be able to answer your questions. I have to go in the ambulance with my friend."

"Okay ma'am thank you." Officer Peters said then walked over to PJ and Jordan. Shy ran out of the room behind the paramedic and got on the back of the ambulance where I was, and we headed to the hospital.

PJ and Jordan were talking but stopped when the two officers approached them.

"Good evening gentlemen." Officer Davis said then reached out to shake their hands, "I just wanted to ask you a few simple questions."

"And I will be writing down everything you say so please be as detailed as you can," Officer Peters said.

"We got you," PJ said.

"Will do," Jordan said.

"So, tell me what happened tonight," Officer Davis said.

"We were all at a party and our homegirl Mariah felt sick so we walked her here to Deon's room."

"Okay who's Mariah and who's Deon?" Officer Davis asked.

"Mariah is the one the ambulance took, and Deon is the guy who murdered our friend Rick last week," PJ answered.

"Okay. Continue," Officer Davis said.

"We got to his room and he wasn't in there so me and PJ left Mariah here, but as we were leaving we ran into Shy; that's the other girl who was just here. We all noticed Deon walking towards his room looking suspicious, so we followed him." Jordan said.

"Yeah he was looking weird as fuck," PJ said then covered his mouth, "Oops, I meant he was looking really weird." He looked at Jordan, "Go head bruh, finish."

"So yeah once we reached the room we stood right here in the front room and overheard Mariah and Deon talking from his room. Apparently, Mariah found some stuff of Rick's in Deon's room and eventually he confessed to being the murderer. Shy called the police at that point and PJ began tussling with Deon after he heard Mariah was in distress. Eventually I had to jump in to help PJ out."

PJ hit Jordan on the arm, "Bruh don't make it seem like he was handling me." He looked at the officers, "look, I lost my footing and had to catch my breath when I hit the ground so he got one up on me but that was it." PJ looked at Jordan who was giving him the side eye, "Okay man I'm just gone stop talking now."

Jordan looked back at the officers, "So like I was saying, in the middle of that, Mariah began yelling for us to stop and she passed out, so we ran to her aid and I told Shy to call the ambulance. She informed us that the police were already on the way, and she made a second 911 call to request an ambulance as well. At that point when Deon heard that the police were on the way, he dipped, and we don't know where he could be honestly."

"PJ chimed in, "But before that weirdo dipped, he head butted me, and I think I need medical attention." He pulled his bottom lip down and showed the officers, "He busted my lip and I think my nose is broken."

Jordan shook his head, "Don't mind him, he's dramatic. We just hope y'all can find Deon as soon as possible though. He's a danger to everyone on campus at this point."

"What does the suspect look like?" Officer Peters asked.

"Weird!" PJ said immediately.

"Man P they serious," Jordan said with disappointment in his voice.

"Me too, hell!" PJ responded.

"Anyways, he is about 5'11, brown skin, kind of husky, and he is wearing a black pull over sweater, gray sweatpants and some black boots," Jordan said.

"Okay, I've written down everything that you both told us. We will begin searching for the suspect immediately. In the meantime, if y'all want to meet your friends at the hospital, you're are free to do so," Officer Peters said.

"Thank you both for your time gentlemen," Officer Davis said.

PJ and Jordan thanked the officers and walked out of Deon's room to the parking lot, then got in Jordan's car and headed to the hospital. While the boys were getting questioned, I was still in the ambulance on the way to the hospital. I opened my eyes a little and my eyesight was slightly blurry; I was able to see Shy and the paramedic leaning over me. I still wasn't able to speak but I was able to move a little, and I could still hear what was going on. I still couldn't really wrap my mind around what took place in Deon's room. A person who I put all my trust into murdered the guy who was like his brother over jealousy. Jealousy killed the father of my child. Jealousy. I laid there and hoped whatever was going on with me that the baby and I would be alright.

"Is she pregnant?" I overheard the paramedic ask Shy.

"Yes, she is eleven weeks," Shy responded.

"The baby may be at high risk for survival," the paramedic said as he grew worried.

I grew worried and wiggled but I still wasn't able to say anything. The paramedic and Shy both did their best to calm me down, but it didn't work because I refused to calm down after hearing that my baby may be at risk. Being that I wouldn't calm down, the paramedic was left with no choice but to sedate me. Not too long after being sedated, we arrived at Perry medical. The paramedic quickly got me out of the ambulance and rolled me inside. My eyes grew heavy and eventually closed, as they rolled me through the hallways of the hospital.

I opened my eyes slowly, and I realized that I was lying in a hospital bed. My eyes grew wide and I quickly leaned up in the bed and started feeling on my stomach through the hospital gown.

My mom walked up on my right, and put her hands on me, "Riah calm down sweetie."

I stopped moving and looked at her, "Mom how's the baby?"

"Honey, the baby is just fine. The baby was a little trooper through the stress and the medication they gave you."

I sighed with relief and leaned back in the bed, "Thank God."

"That baby is tough like its God mama," Shy said from the left of me.

I turned my head in the direction of her voice and saw her sitting on the couch with PJ and Jordan. Shy had on a tank top and jeans with flip flops, PJ and Jordan both had on Perry University basketball shirts, sweatpants and slides.

I smiled at all them, "Hey y'all."

"Hey girl," Shy said.

"Sup sis," PJ said.

"Hey sis, how you feeling?" Jordan asked.

"Much better, thank you Jordan. And thank you PJ."

"All love sis," PJ responded.

"We gave you our word to always be there for you and we meant that," Jordan added.

I smiled again, "I appreciate it so much."

"Hey sweetie," My dad said from the right.

I turned and looked in that direction and saw him dressed casually sitting in the chair, and I saw Mr. Fuller standing next to him in his work clothes.

"Hey dad. Hey pops."

"Hey Riah. Glad you are doing good," Mr. Fuller said then he walked over to me and gave me a hug.

"Thank you pops."

"No problem sweetie."

We stopped hugging as there was a knock on the room door. The doctor walked in; he was a tall and skinny white man, with black hair.

"Good morning everyone, my name is Doctor White." Everyone said good morning back, then he made his way over to me, "Hello Mrs. Jones, how are you feeling?"

"I am doing better than I was last night," I responded.

"Great! Well thankfully there's nothing severely wrong. You were just dehydrated and a little stressed out. We checked to see if the baby was okay and it is looking healthy and doing just fine. Like I mentioned before, there aren't any major concerns, but please stay hydrated and try to keep your stress levels at a minimum, especially since you are expecting."

"Yes sir, I will thank you."

"I know your mom will stay on top of you. She keeps most of us in line around here," he chuckled.

My mom chuckled, "Somebody has too."

"You're right," he chuckled, "Well I will be back to check on you a little later. Just let me know if you need anything."

"Okay, I will."

"Alrighty. Have a good one everyone."

Everyone said bye to him, and he walked out of the room and closed the door behind him.

"Hey, everyone. Do y'all mind if I turn on the TV real quick? I just want to check the scores of the games from yesterday." PJ said.

"Go head baby," my mom said.

PJ grabbed the remote off of the table, and turned on the TV. PJ was about to change the channel from the local news station.

"Wait!" I yelled out and sat up in the bed, "Is that Deon's mug shot on the screen?"

Jordan stood up off of the couch and walked towards the TV, "That is him." He grabbed the remote from PJ and turned the TV up.

"Late last night Deon Bradley was arrested for the murder of Richard Fuller. It has been confirmed that he will be charged with premeditated murder, first degree murder, obstruction of evidence and fleeing from the police. We have no further information other than that the trial should be held early next week. Our condolences go out to the Fuller family once again," said the News Broadcaster.

"They got his ass!" PJ said then covered his mouth as he looked at the adults in the room, "Excuse my language."

Mr. Fuller walked towards the TV, "He killed my boy." He turned and looked at me in the bed, "Did you know this? Is this the reason why you passed out from stress last night?"

"Yes. I was just as shocked when I found out it was Deon last night. It was so much to take in at one time, and I guess my mind couldn't handle it."

"Yeah Mr. Fuller, we all kind of found out at the same time last night. If we didn't find out the way we did, we probably wouldn't have ever found out the truth, honestly," Shy added.

"How could Deon do something like that?" My dad asked in a disappointed voice.

My mom covered her mouth, "I just can't believe this."

Mr. Fuller's eyes started to water, "I'm sorry, I need to step out for a minute. He walked out of the room door.

"I'm going to go out and check on him," my dad said as he followed behind Mr. Fuller. Everyone else in the room was glad that Deon was caught, while my mom still sat in disbelief.

I rubbed my stomach and looked at Shy, PJ and Jordan, "I really thank y'all because if it wasn't for you, Deon would still be free and Rick's murder would have went unsolved."

"Yeah we had to give him that work, I know my boy Rick is proud of how we handled things," PJ responded first.

Yeah, I would've never guessed it was Deon though. But I'm just glad we solved this thing so Rick can now rest in peace," Jordan said.

"Exactly," Shy said.

"Baby, I'm just in disbelief, you know I looked at Deon as one of my children, so for him to do this just doesn't make sense to me. Why, why would he do this?" my mom asked.

Shy looked at my mom, "Jealousy, Mrs. Jones."

I sighed deeply, "Yeah, jealousy was a part of it, but he primarily fell victim to indignation."

Everyone looked at me and nodded in agreement.

2018

A year has now gone by and so much has changed. June of this year I gave birth to a beautiful baby girl named Jasmine Allice Fuller, I named her after Rick's mom. My baby girl looks so much like her father and that means the world to me. I decided to move back home with my parents, and I've transferred from Livingston to Perry. I am now going to school part-time. My parents and Mr. Fuller love and adore Jasmine so much; they do everything they can to make raising her easier for me. Mr. Fuller began working less and started living life again. He began to travel and became more social. He eventually opened back up and found time to find love again.

Shy changed her major from nursing to cosmetology and works at a local hair studio. Her parents supported her decision fully, and they often tell her that they're happy that she's pursuing a career in the field of what she loves to do. Surprisingly, Shy finally decided to give love a try, all thanks to me. I convinced her to stop being a hard body and give PJ a chance, and I've never seen her happier. Of course, Lacy didn't like the fact that PJ moved on from her, but Shy nipped that in the bud real quick; we haven't seen Lacy since her last altercation with Shy. As for PJ, he dropped the basketball team and decided to focus strictly on school. No one knows what he's majoring in though, I don't even think he knows.

Everyone eventually forgave Lamar, he gave up the street life and focused on the more important things in life like school, friendship and loyalty. He and Jordan are still on the team and as of last season they're now the top two players on the team. They took the team to the national championship last year but unfortunately, they didn't win. But I'm sure this year they will win, hands down!

Even though Avery had nothing to do with Rick's murder, word got out that he had plans to plot against Rick. That caused nearly the entire campus to beef with him. Who would've thought so many people loved Rick like that. Even Avery's own boys turned against him just to avoid backlash from everyone else. A little after Thanksgiving of last year he was arrested for armed robbery. No one kept tabs on him after that, so he hasn't been seen since.

We haven't seen either of the Bradley's since Rick's funeral, my mom hasn't even seen Mrs. Bradley at work. They kind of fell off of the radar, especially after the news about Deon got out to the public. You would think they would at least check on us even though it was obvious we didn't consider Deon a friend anymore, but oh well. As for Deon, he didn't last long in jail. Word got out that he was in for the murder of Rick. Some of Rick's old gang members were locked up in the same jail as Deon and made every day a living hell for him. Rumor has it that Deon committed suicide, but I think we all know what really happened.

Life has gotten easier day by day living without Rick, but it'll never be the same. I will make it a priority to make Rick proud and let his legacy live on through Jasmine and all of those who loved him. I will also make sure Jasmine knows all about how her father and I met and came to be. I frequently take her to the park in the neighborhood where my parents and I live. We always sit on the same bench on the side of the basketball court where Rick and I first met.

ACKNOWLEDGE-MENTS

I have been blessed to be surrounded by a group of intelligent and supportive people who have helped me turn a crazy idea into the book that you are now holding.

My first thank you goes out to Nailah Crawford. She is my best friend who attended Armstrong State University with me. After I explained the idea to her, she helped me get my creative juices flowing, and even added a few ideas in herself. We spent long nights on the phone just thinking about what we could add to this work, so that people would enjoy reading.

I would like to offer my immense appreciation to "The Crew", my best friends from my hometown who I have been friends with since elementary school. I consider Marcavius Dudley, David Frazier, Danicia Ramsey, Carmen Burns, Nakiah Parrish, Shikara Carroll, and Dominique Cooper my brothers and sisters. From the beginning since the first draft, they were very open with their feedback and constructive criticism, and for that, I thank each of them dearly.

A BIG thank you goes to my mom, Lakisha Williams, who was also amongst the first to have the opportunity to read the script. She always told me how proud she was of my work, and I can't thank her enough for her continuous support on everything that I have accomplished thus far.

I would like to extend a big thank you to another best friend of mine from Armstrong, Daeja Colquitt. We spent many days and night working hard to convert my initial script into book format.

It was easier said than done, but we stayed the course. I really can't thank Daeja enough for all the consistent help she has provided me during this writing and publishing process to get this book (my first of many) to its final product and out to the public.

A very good friend of mine, Steven Ralston, who I really consider an older brother, assisted me getting my book copyrighted. Steve invested in me in multiple ways, as he saw how hard I was working on this. He read the book carefully, going through it with me page by page offering valuable ideas, suggestions, as well as offering different points of view. Steve deserves a big thank you for the help he has provided to me during this publishing process.

I would like to thank my sister, Takeyah Taylor, and my line brother, William Johnson, for the time and effort they each put into the eBook and paperback covers of this book. I am immensely grateful to them both.

And if you are reading this, thank you so very much for purchasing this book and supporting me. You are very much appreciated, and I am forever grateful that you chose to purchase this book. I am humbled and blessed by your generosity. Thank you, thank you, thank you!

~Be on the lookout for my next book, *Shooting Starr,* which should be coming to an Amazon near you in 2020.

ABOUT THE AUTHOR

Anthony Deshawn Taylor, who some know as "Fresh", was born and raised in Brunswick, GA. In June of 2009, at the age of 16, Anthony began having trouble with his vision. By October of that year, was diagnosed with Leber's Hereditary Optic Neuropathy, and as a result, he became completely blind. This major change would shape and change him in ways that were indescribable. Even now, ten years later, the thought of never being able to see again sometimes still feels unreal.

Although the loss of his sight presented major challenges, it has not deterred him from striving to achieve lifelong goals, while continuing to set new ones. Shortly after graduating high school in May 2010, Anthony attended the Savannah Association for the Blind (now known as Savannah Center for Blind and Low Vision) where he learned skills to prepare him for college and life after college. In fall 2011, Anthony enrolled at The College of Costal Georgia. In the spring of 2015, Anthony transferred to Armstrong State University (now known as Georgia Southern University), where he helped charter the Alpha Delta Alpha Chapter of Omega Psi Phi Fraternity Inc. In December of 2017, Anthony graduated with a bachelor's degree in English Professional Communication.

Indignation is his first novel, and he's spent countless nights on this work. Anthony never thought that a young, blind man from a small country town in South Georgia would be the author of a published novel. This journey has taught Anthony a lot, and he is so humbled and grateful for valuable lessons he's learned along the way. To complete his first book is a huge accomplishment, and dream come true for him. Although this is his first novel, Anthony intends to write many more, and has already began writing

Anthony Taylor

his next two novels.

Made in the USA
Columbia, SC
20 August 2019